ABOUT THE WRITER

SYLVIA V. LINSTEADT is a writer and artist based in California. Her collection of stories, *The Gray Fox Epistles*, won the James D. Phelan Literary Award from the San Francisco Foundation in 2014. Her other books include *The Wild Folk* – which was nominated for the 2019 CILIP Carnegie Medal – *The Wild Folk Rising* and *Our Lady of the Dark Country*.

ABOUT THE PAINTER

RIMA STAINES was born in London in 1979 to a family of artists. Her book illustration work includes *The Irresistible Fairytale: The Cultural and Social History of a Genre* by Jack Zipes, *Baba Yaga: The Wild Witch of the East in Russian Fairy Tales* by Sibelan Forrester et al., Catherynne M. Valente's *Ventriloquism* and *Sometimes a Wild God* by her partner Tom Hirons. Her paintings have been exhibited in the UK, France, the USA and New Zealand. Rima and Tom live with their two young sons in Devon, UK, where they run Hedgespoken – a small press and travelling storytelling theatre.

A novel by SYLVIA V. LINSTEADT

With paintings by RIMA STAINES

First published in 2017
This paperback edition first published in 2021

Unbound
Level 1, Devonshire House,
One Mayfair Place, London W1J 8AJ
unbound.com

All rights reserved

© Sylvia V. Linsteadt & Rima Staines, 2017

The right of Sylvia V. Linsteadt & Rima Staines to be identified as the author and artist of this work has been asserted in accordance with Section 77 of the Copyright, Designs and Patents Act 1988.

No part of this publication may be copied, reproduced, stored in a retrieval system, or transmitted, in any form or by any means without the prior permission of the publisher, nor be otherwise circulated in any form of binding or cover other than that in which it is published and without a similar condition being imposed on the subsequent purchaser.

Text design by Patty Rennie
Hand-drawn lettering by Rima Staines
Art direction by Mark Ecob

A CIP record for this book is available from the British Library

ISBN 978-1-78352-956-8 (trade pbk)
ISBN 978-1-78352-329-0 (trade hbk)
ISBN 978-1-78352-330-6 (ebook)
ISBN 978-1-78352-331-3 (limited edition)

Printed in Slovenia by DZS

1 3 5 7 9 8 6 4 2

FOR THE ONES WHO CAME BEFORE
AND THE ONES WHO ARE TO COME:
MAY THE EARTH RISE UP IN OUR WORDS
AND PAINTINGS AND SONGS. MAY WE
TELL THE WAY BACK HOME.

TIME LINE

BEFORE — PRESENT TO 2025 CE
(Rose, The Holy Beggars)

THE FALL — 2025 TO 2043 CE
(Margaret)

THE CAMPS — 2044–2198 CE
(Wheel, Martin)

THE FOOL'S REVOLT — 2198 CE
(Wheel, Iris, Ffion, Martin)

THE WILD FOLK — 2198–2315 CE
(Anja, Bells, Perches & Boots, Molly, Poppy)

The Beginning
2315 CE

EVEN THE RAVENS STOPPED THE GLOSS OF THEIR CROAKING CALLS UP over the fir trees when the boy Poppy began to speak aloud. He read words from a book made of gray leather. The book was held in the hands of the wheeled creature called Lyoobov. On her great arched back, taller than any horse, sat a barn owl who listened with round yellow eyes.

Before, watching from the needled bows and last scraps of telephone wires, the ravens had known Poppy as the boy, quick and orange-haired, who could speak in their velvet tones, who looked like a person but had the blood of a wild thing nursed on fir sap, on brush rabbit livers and black walnuts. They had known him as that fiery streak of loneliness, cawing and whistling and hissing as he went, no human word in him, wanting to touch every last thing he saw, even their own black feathers, which they once, in a startle of pity, let him do. They had known him as the little person with the shiny battered coffeepot, always polished, that he had found half-buried in sand on the beach and kept with him always, for brewing up dirt and thimbleberries, yerba buena leaves, the poppies of his name, over small fires. He poured his concoctions into acorn caps or buckeye shells and fed them to passing creatures—harvest mice, foxes, snakes, warblers. Always, whatever he poured in turned into the thing most needed—grass seeds, blood, mosquito-hawk legs.

Now, he made his voice human as he read from the pages of that big book. The ravens gathered overhead as below the people from the hamlet called Nettleburn crowded close. They all kept the distance, still, that you would from a bonfire, as if Lyoobov or Poppy were coals. Even so, old men with braids in their white beards, with missing fingers and battered vests that still held a little of their original red, reached toward Lyoobov like she would warm them. Lyoobov was supposed to be only a story, dead for three hundred years. They were weeping.

Molly, the mother of Poppy, stood in her husband's arms with tears all over her own cheeks that had joy and also grief in them. Joy because her Poppy had been gone three years and she had been sure he was dead. He'd left on a July afternoon during his fourteenth year with a bag full of rosemary cakes, the battered old coffeepot he took everywhere, and a little green marble in his hand, heading toward the creek where he always went to watch for newts. He hadn't returned. Joy because she had never before heard him speak a word in any human tongue. Grief because he leaned into Lyoobov's chest like he had found a home, because he spoke now, when he had never spoken at her urging. This, she knew, was his real mother, this strange and wheeled beast they all had thought belonged only to the myths of a distant Fall. Lyoobov was luminous as any planet, and Molly's boy swooned, at home in that orbit.

Poppy's voice as he read was strong and only a little accented, not with the lilt of another version of English or Spanish, no, but rather with the languages of streams moving, of ravens chortling and mountain lions purring to their kittens. Every so often a choke or a yip or hiss entered his speaking, and the people gathering, and gathering found that they could not look away. Nor did they want to look away from that boy and that big wheeling beast. His odd voice echoed outward as he leaned back into the glowing Lyoobov, who seemed to be lantern-lit from within.

Poppy read only in the strictest sense of the word. It was as if, the old men whispered to the old women as they lit up pipes of cured tobacco and brought out candied hazelnuts saved for years for some outstanding occasion, it was as if he only had a voice when he put his eyes upon the book in Lyoobov's hands. Otherwise his words would have been all towhee-speak. There on those pages the words formed and gathered. Those pages were his mind, his soul, they whispered, and Lyoobov his translator. And really they weren't pages at all, but bark-bound sheaves of a body scratched with bird tracks and woodpecker holes.

Poppy

I'VE A FOX-SWALLOWED HEART I DO. IT WAS MADE UNDERGROUND, you see, in the ribs of Lyoobov, who has known gunfire but has regrown like any wise plant will do from her waiting roots. The only difference is that this Lyoobov came back as a female, not a male, like plants that have both the ovum and the pollen. Red alder trees for example. She found that was easiest. She found it was necessary, this time, to be a she instead of a he. A mama-beast, not a papa-beast.

Of course you want to know that story of resurrection, but I'm not much of an alchemist. I know nothing of the metaphysical. I know only that I walked because I was looking for newts but I found no newts in the creek, so I walked further, and further, and I seemed to have some fire in my soles so I kept going. It was like following a red string or the path of a doe and all of her arrowed hoofprint. I walked and ate rosemary cakes from my mother. The stellar's jays cackled, flaunting their black combs and spreading flashes of indigo with their wings in the oaks. I poured them perfect worms from my coffeepot and they quieted down. They even left me a handful of blue feathers, which I put in my hair.

My need to keep on walking was like what you're filled with when you meet a pretty girl and something about her is a whole hillside of purple lupines in your blood and you can't do anything except hold her in your mind's hands and follow wherever she goes. I know you think because I never could speak to you your way that I was simple or dumb or made in the wrong body with longings only for coyote-girls or something, but you are all mistaken. I have loved quietly like any boy. Annabelle, yes, I see you there turning pink because you remember how I watched you through the window of your father's place where he fixed up all our shoes with tree resin and old rubber from the beach, string from the guts of rats. It was like that, the feeling as I walked for days—that kind of longing, that need for wholeness. I barely ate besides the rosemary cakes and new huckleberries in the woods, tart ones that made my tongue dry.

At the end of my walking, Lyoobov and I just found each other, in the middle of a field made all of tar broken in fissures and veins by a thousand thick dandelions and milk thistles and clusters of fennel. It was like Lyoobov had been there all along, my whole life singing my small name, *Poppy, Poppy,* to the wind in thousands and thousands of small seeds.

We are parts of the same thing, she and I. I am hers and she is mine. Lyoobov is not the same as before, not quite, because her bones came apart and then reassembled and she had to grow ligaments, veins, skin, which the broad-footed moles helped with.

She told me that all the barn owls gathered blood from their prey in their beaks until there was enough to fill her whole body. Her heart grew from iris tubers, from a thousand million lacey pieces of mycelium knitting and knitting at all the last red thimbleberries and freshly dead fox hearts of that great meadow where she was buried as a he hundreds of years ago by the woman named Margaret who had watched him die. Before, Lyoobov was the map through the World as They Knew It and Out the Other Side, and he was a boy, like me. Now, Lyoobov, she is a Maker, that's what she says, and so she is a girl.

Listen: I rode on the back of Lyoobov all the way east up the big mountains to where the snow starts and the sun rises and the clouds drop everything and the waters flow down.

Listen: I can tell you what happened to Anja, whose name you are always murmuring. *Anja protect my child, Anja bless this bread, Anja heal this wound.*

I can tell you her story. We are carrying it, me in my little chest-country, Lyoobov in the great chamber of her abdomen which I have slept in through a small trapdoor beneath her.

But listen: all stories are hitched to a hundred others like spokes on wheels. We told stories, catching up, dreaming of bright lines through the sky that hitched us to each other, that splintered and shone through our identical bones. We are carrying voices from Before. All the threads that made Lyoobov, that made Anja, that made me.

It's all candle-lit and red inside of Lyoobov, and she has been keeping these Stories safe too beside the heating hearth of her heart, where my coffeepot rests, near to boiling, ready to pour. You'd never believe it, what my pot brews on the hearth of Lyoobov's heart.

You are whispering loud, you are coming closer. Yes, I do mean Anja born of the buckeye whose mother was Wheel. Yes, like Bells, Perches and Boots have told it, kestrel-watched, cowbell-clanged, sole-trod. I don't know how to tell a thing like they do. I only know how to say it all fox-swallowed and then spat up again with fur and bones on these pages which are and are not like new white milkmaid flowers perpetually blossoming and then dropping their petals all over our feet, growing with their roots right in Lyoobov's ribcage, where I was, after all, born.

I will tell it all to you, the life of Anja. But I will have to tell you from the beginning, Before the Fall.

First, I will tell you how we came to know any of this at all.

It started out that we were just rolling along the broken highways of the Valley that stretches forever and ever, out to squares with overgrown orchards of fruit trees dry and dead. The Valley is scattered with empty canals, silt and crabgrass thrusting up everywhere. We picked fruit at first, until the orchards grew crippled, twisted, like they'd been poisoned.

Lyoobov crooned to me each morning that it was time to go East, toward the sunrise and the place where the snow all gathers up those granite peaks. That's where it all Began, she said to me, in her way. That's where she had first been dreamed into being four centuries ago, cold in the foothills in the snow, under the sky full of the smog that drifted and stayed from a City to the west.

Lyoobov trundled on, murmuring about ice up in the mountains, and I followed, teaching myself to juggle shriveled almonds and peaches from the trees at the western edge of the Valley, boiling them up later in my coffeepot and pouring out vials of some elixir for the two of us, nothing transformed—just the hot syrup of peach and ground up almond.

One morning, we found an orchard empty of leaves or fruits, and wandered between the endless trunks of the almond trees, horrified, wondering at this desolation. There, we met a woman.

That's when it truly began.

From far away, coming through the trunks, she looked like a girl my age, tanned as a nut, tangled bun of hair, long moving skirts of tawny fabric stained and frayed but so ample it was hard to tell exactly where they ended. Close up, her face was lined a thousand ways like the little feet of songbirds. She greeted us with a hand raised. She smiled at me specifically, brilliantly, so that her whole face moved. To Lyoobov she nodded, a low nod almost like a bow, and she said:

"You're up and lurching around already, that's a good start." She reached a hand to lift her skirt to her ankles and I saw a sea of sparrow, junco, finch, wrentit and kinglet feet around her own feet, pecking at a ground as vast as the whole Valley. She grabbed one, a yellow goldfinch, snapped its neck and split it open with a single long fingernail.

"Here is a map of the way up the mountains. You knew already, didn't you Lyoobov, that somebody's been calling, hard to say who, somebody's been dreaming and time to go back, like a blue thread on a needle stitching a single blue stitch up there and leaving the line between so that the place the water comes from and the place it goes are one, not a clogged artery all laced up with sorrow."

"Iris from the stories!" I said, and it came out a garble of these words from Lyoobov's book and the speaking of songbirds. My head went light with the feeling of it, of human words coming from my tongue, all sharp and tender at the same time. I reached out my hands to cradle that little goldfinch, the color of poppy pollen and the dark shade of night, still warm, still with a cheep in his beak, a word of comfort, a word of satisfaction at a small worm. Inside his opened abdomen, ribs as fine as plant stalks, I saw the sharp granite and snow and blue riverbeds of the mountains called the Sierra Nevada, looming to the east. The ones we'd already been moving toward. I saw the whole mountain range in there and I also saw a fine tracery of paths, magnified. The amount of detail that yellow-feathered body contained made my head spin.

Iris grinned at me like a girl and it made her face complicated, an old woman's rivuleted topography of skin.

"Mmm," she said. "I have been called that." A wink. "Follow the blue creeks. I think you'll get to the right place eventually, between the two of you." She pulled several dried up bird organs the size of fingernails from a pocket and ate them like berries. "And you," she said, touching my red hair, "listen well."

After she left I wished I'd offered her a draught from my coffeepot; I wanted to know what would have poured out. What it was she needed most. Perhaps it was best I didn't.

The dead almond trees and the patches of crabgrass turned to broken tar, the ghost-bones of suburban houses, and dust, as we went further East over that Valley. Dust and fallow fields with stumps of old life across them, little husks and withered root balls. Poisoned, I whispered to Lyoobov and she whispered to me, and below our feet we could feel the sorrows of buried rivers, long ago dammed and dug under in tunnels of cement. By the time we rolled into the dry juniper scrub foothills, me sitting up on Lyoobov's broad back with the blossomed book of her bones in my hands, learning and learning its sounds, the sounds of my boy's voice as a thing separate from a raven's, a frog's, a streambed's.

Lyoobov always made the fire. It was an extraordinary thing to watch her gray leathery hands, her nimble wheeled bulk, her short trunk and her tail and her big dark eyes like cut out moons with tapered edges—all of her went into the making of a blaze. It was like she was giving birth to it, stick by gathered stick, tented into perfect forms that allowed the air and the flames to twine and crackle and sear. Afterward, she ate the embers, one by one, savoring.

Every night I held out that dissected goldfinch for us to peer inside of. It never seemed to decompose, only remained a just-dead yellow form, neck broken, changed from a body to a map. We followed the blue lines like veins in the mountain range of her ribcage, not because we had any idea what we would find, but because it felt like the only thing in the world to do. It felt like following sustenance; like this was the only way to be fed, though we ate haphazardly—quail and lizards, roots, almonds stored in Lyoobov's carriage-sized middle. I slept there nightly, the embers she had eaten warming her body, part wagon, part beast she is, a place all made for dreaming in.

It may have been a year, a year and a half, it took us to get there. I cannot say. We rolled, we dreamed, through that wasteland of dust, up the mountain. We changed and we also stayed much as we always had been.

When the air got thin in my lungs and dry, and Lyoobov had to slow her wheeling between the cream and pollen colors of the granite, the tall straight pines redolent of some burnt sweetness, I smelled the fires of other people. It had been a long time since I had smelled the fires of other people. I saw places on the ground smudged with footprints made by wide thick soles. I saw the tracks of deer too, a black bear, all mixed in, a great shifting pattern, and I grew uneasy. So many animal tracks. We have creatures here, near Nettleburn, but they are very shy. They hide from us. Well, from you, not from me. They still do not trust you. Here, there were tracks everywhere, even ones like a mountain lion makes.

Up on the top of the next ridge, I saw a tall metal set of poles and bars, a black square with a little box on top with windows, and two sets of cables heading down toward us, then trailing off into the stones and grasses. The box on top was grown everywhere with a fringe of grass and columbine flowers, all scarlet and orange. I saw a face in the broken window, a young woman's, hair in a coiled black mat on top of her head, skin like the darkness of the soil where my mother pulled me out. A bird flashed out the broken window, a jay, calling the way they do to warn of bobcats sneaking in the underbrush. The woman climbed fast as any red-furred squirrel, down a dark pole, and came toward us. I leaned into Lyoobov's shoulder and she rustled her trunked nose against my hair, breathing out a warm breath that smelled of earth and firelight and comfort.

I held out the opened body of the goldfinch as the woman came to stand before us, weeping tears that moved blue against her dark cheeks, at the sight of Lyoobov.

"You've found us," she said. "Nobody finds us but the ones we want. Which has been nobody, no, not anybody but you." She said this to Lyoobov, touching her trunk. Her hair, close up, was a dense forest, felted like wool is felted, rope after rope and twined with green lace lichen, teeth of tiny bear cubs, a red plastic string from some far away kitchen. Such things hold their color almost forever.

"We don't know what we're here for," said Lyoobov, said I, through the petaled pages of her book. The woman smiled. She took the goldfinch in her hands and tucked it deep into the folds of her hair.

"Come along," she said.

Lyoobov rolled, the crunching of granite dust, and I walked, leaning into her because I knew that she knew how to be brave among strangers. Her leathery skin smelled of honey and dust after rain. It soothed me. We followed the woman who introduced herself as Sare. I watched the dirt and found that when she walked she did not leave the footprints of a woman, but rather those of a small bear. The red plastic cord in her hair glinted like a line of blood. I still couldn't tell you if the feeling in me, in my chest, under my ribs, was fear or joy.

Moving all dark as bearfur and smooth as honey from wild hives, Sare took us higher and over a ridge of granite. It was like a big torn-up spine, ancient and bare to the sharp blue sky. When we crossed it, I felt the way your ears do slipping into a lake: dark green and deep, newts showing you their orange bellies all around like moving candleflames. My head felt thick. The trees became twisted around us, wind-made, thin, wending between smooth granite once licked by the great tongues of glaciers. Shadows moved across the stone ground in whorls like birds were passing in front of the sun, but it was only those curved trees, silver-barked, resinous.

Suddenly there were small circular structures through the trees made of bone. A man wearing a marmot-fur hat hung strips of fish to smoke over a fire. I thought this was a village of Wild Folk, not people at all, living not just bear-women alone but all mixed. Even the trees—lodgepole, white pine, juniper—they seemed to look out from their bark. I watched for slender men to unfurl from their trunks but none did. I didn't feel afraid because they are more like me than you are—the woodrat women out in the scrub who have every last fallen coin (pennies, dimes, nickels, quarters), the small robin men in woodlands who ask that you sing up the worms. I know them though you are afraid and run after you leave them the requisite eggs, buttons, scraps of dream.

Each hut, I saw, was made all of one kind of bone—entirely crow, entirely deer, entirely weasel. The structures were pale as snow.

When the people there saw us arrive, the day became all at once a flood of feasting, a flood of those people who kept murmuring the name Anja, and quieter, Lyoobov.

"No one here from down there across the Valley to the Bay, not since Anja, Anja and her man. Anja, Anja."

It became a chant into the smoke of a dozen juniper-wood fires where a deer was roasted, and lily bulbs, and wild onions, and these people, they all gathered, dressed in soft wools and soft skins. They were only people, not Wild Folk, I saw: the way their eyes rested gently on me, on Lyoobov, taking us in the way people take in other people, which is very different than a raccoon or a woman with egret wings and egret legs, who read you for the layers of you under your skin.

They knew to feed Lyoobov hot embers, glowing as if they were apricots on fire; they knew that this was her favorite food, that she would smoke through her ears and the shape of those tendrils would rise up in the form of lost alphabets, which curved and moved like vines, hoofprint, the branches of trees. Those tendrils made me wonder if maybe all words, all languages, like the ones I know best from the teeth of the moles and the fir boughs, have been absorbed back into the dirt or the plum pits or the bellies of mountain lions, but are not all the way gone.

At one point in the evening, as someone passed around thimbleberry mead and the fires moved hotly with the shapes of wild mustangs and condors, Sare touched my shoulder and she said, "Your bird, your little goldfinch map, yellow as a lemon, she has the seed of Anja in her liver." Between her thumb and forefinger she held up a small red bead. It matched the plastic red string in her hair.

"I don't know much about Anja. I didn't really listen to human stories, when I was small," I said to her, but I said it the way black bears speak, which I learned from the beehives that remembered the cadence of those dark muzzles that once came romping down through the woods. She paused.

A red flush moved through her cheeks the color of earth. She fidgeted her fingers on the bead, looked to see if anyone had heard—looked at the man who had been smoking fish when we arrived, her father.

"No, but you will, and more besides. You'll get to know her very roots," she replied in human words. Then added, bear-touched but soft as a whisper: "there's an old Juniper, said she told her story to it like a person to another person. Under the bark. I'll bet you can get the words out. I think she told it for someone of your kind to come and to hear." She handed me the red bead, and then a tiny bear claw from her hair.

I went alone. Nobody noticed me going. I had just my silver coffeepot hitched on a string over my back, like always. Lyoobov stayed, eating the embers one by one, letting smoke spell poems into the night from her coiled trunk, her ears. She let the women come and rub her gray skin with the oils of pine nuts and wildflower essences. The shadows from the fire leapt onto the wind-shaped pines. I held that red seed and I walked through the dark, feeling ahead with my feet.

It wasn't hard to find the tree Sare meant because it was ancient and its trunk silver as all the stars, as time. The hard blue-dusted berries were thick, everywhere, a thousand blue earths. I picked up handfuls and stuck them through the top of my coffeepot. The whole tree in my ears thundered like a fast heart. It creaked in the wind. It wanted me near, under the rounded spires of branch, up to the trunk, my body a warmth to keep company through the night. I set the red bead into a crease of the trunk. I smelled the bark. I found that to the left of my feet, in the shadows, was a darker shadow, like a hole. I crawled to see and it was just as wide as my shoulders, gaping, darker than any night can be dark. I went in because Sare told me that I would be able to hear the stories and bring them back.

I've wanted, I've always wanted, to do one single thing you all approved of.

The bear tooth Sare gave me glowed. I saw the inside of that Juniper. Time had carved waterways of lines, the color soft as firelight or amber. The patterns of stars seemed to be glinting wherever I looked in that hollow of bark, which went deep down below in root tunnels, and up further than that glowing tooth could shed light. That's when the voice started. It unpeeled from the layers of bark and echoed. It was, and was not, human. It was juniper berry blue in my mind where I held it as it spoke, in my hands where I felt it, dusty, weathered. Steeped and smoked with the centuries of Juniper growing, Juniper seeking water, Juniper breathing and releasing the thin air. It was her, the tree, whispering.

"Little child," came that voice, and a smell of soft smoke. "Little child. You are only a little child." All along the inner bark, stars gleamed, in familiar and unfamiliar constellations, from the old stories which I had never before understood—the one in the shape of a wheel which we call Wheel, after the long ago Fool; the one like an owl, for Margaret, with a bell in its claws; the one like a fiddle, for Rose; the tiny cluster, for the Holy Beggars. And more, gleaming and shifting all around me, ones I couldn't name. I felt I might have clambered into the beginning of a world.

"I'm Poppy," I said, deep inside the tree now, in a ruckled chamber whorled with bark. "I am little, it's true."

"You have come to learn the true story of Anja." This time, the voice was nearer, and I turned. In the shadows, on the walls of her trunk, was a woman. She was all hunched up, rounded like the blue berries I'd stuffed into my silver coffeepot. Then she seemed to peel right off the wall, a dark shade. She came and she sat opposite me. In the glow of the juniper bark around us, I saw an ancient little lady with a dozen spindly arms lined as juniper branches, with a spiking mass of hair like spired juniper needles. White hairs grew on her chin. Her eyes were all patched with cataracts, but she had a good set of teeth. I noticed this, I don't know why, maybe because they flashed.

"Yes," I stammered.

"But do you even know your own?"

"Well enough," I replied, staring into my coffeepot because her eyes were too strange, and milky. "My mother found me in the earth, only really I am part of Lyoobov, and Lyoobov is part of me—"

"But who is Lyoobov, and how, and why?"

"Lyoobov was born out of the dream of Rose, a long time ago, Before the Fall. But what have I got to do with Anja?"

"You were there at the beginning, because Lyoobov was there. You are here now, at the end. But what about the middle, little child, little Poppy, little heart? How can you ask for Anja, without everything that came before? How can you know a whole world, without every tattered thread?"

The silvery bark of the juniper's inner trunk was shifting, the stars scattered there wheeling, like they might across a whole night, not a single moment. I had no words at all.

"Did you know that some stars are only memories of light, already dead? Like the voices of people, echoing long after they are gone?"

There were figures coalescing against the bark, the way the Juniper-woman's had, ghosts that one by one peeled away, edged in stars. Rose. The Holy Beggars. St. Margaret, with owl wings. Wheel. Martin. Ffion.

"When you hear a story, little child, it has been folded and unfolded a hundred times in the mouths of its tellers. But the truest stories come right from the source."

The starry ghosts gathered, and waited, glinting.

One by one, they told their tales, just pieces of them, the way people do. You don't remember your whole life all at once. If someone asks you to tell a story, it turns around a central point, a moment or a day or a loss. I sat, and listened, and into my coffeepot, beside the juniper berries, fell the voices of stars, which were also ghosts, and long ago, people.

Constellation I

a girl mad
as birds

Before, & the Fall

2015 – 2043 CE

•

Rose

THEY ALWAYS SAID THE GIRL WAS AS MAD AS BIRDS WHEN SHE CAME into town for a cup of coffee, a sack of licorice chews. They said you could hear her talking under her breath, and when you stood close, it wasn't a human sound at all, but a broken, high chirping. No one knew where she lived, if it was up the hill and past the place where the asphalt streets and the houses stopped, into the scrub and the forest: lupine, madrone, oak. Now and then a woman slipping her shoes on at the front porch saw the girl come down from the mountain fire-road at dawn, oak leaves in her hair. At school, the children whispered that she lived underground, in the roots of trees, or maybe under their parents' cars, in the dark small places that couldn't be seen. The boutique owners busily swept their doorsteps when she passed by in the same linen dress, the same long-sleeved undershirt, day after day. Her dress always dragged its wide hem and collected dirt. The owner of the kitchen-supply store complained that she left a highway of birdshit on the sidewalk in her wake, because all the downtown pigeons, all the little blackbirds, they liked to fly after her and land on her shoulders or in her hair. There was only one man at the coffeeshop who would let her in and serve her a cup. He worked on Tuesday and Thursday mornings, so that's when she came, making sing-song cheeps under her breath. His family had come from another place, and his skin was not the same color as everyone else's, so he knew, he whispered to her over the cash register, handing her change, what it was like to not be allowed to belong.

I was the only one who knew her secret, because I was the only one who smiled and watched her without feeling afraid, without feeling tight in my stomach and stiff in my neck. Sometimes, that's all it takes to see more clearly, to see the things that have been there all along. Often, this is the province of children, before they've learned to believe that people have souls and birds do not.

I knew that she had birds under her long skirt. The kind that feed on the ground: towhees, dark-headed juncos, chickadees, sparrows. The humble birds, all simple feathered browns and blacks, the kinds everyone forgets. They bustled along with her everywhere, held in the dark shadow of her dress, chittering and feeding on street crumbs and the bits of rosehip or blackberry she now and then dropped from her fingers. That's who she talked to in high chirrups. The edges of her dress moved with their small, feathered forms, so many of them around her that I imagined an impossibly ample space in the dark shadow of her skirt: scrub and nest and forest, all there in the darkness of her legs.

They weren't pretty birds. Maybe that's why no one noticed them: no one looked long enough to see them. They were battered—a towhee with a nick in her wing, a junco with a crooked beak, a white crowned sparrow with a missing foot. They were shabby, like her—tousled and threadbare and worn in. That's why I followed her home one Thursday afternoon. I snuck right out of the schoolyard at recess. I wasn't afraid. It was a gentle shabbiness, and she didn't look that much older than me, even though she was threadbare. That day, I was eleven. I still liked to build mud-dams across the creek, with sticks for towers and ivy leaves for flags. The other girls sat in the corner together and laughed about bras.

I followed her up the path with brick steps that led out of downtown. It wound between houses, straight up hill, one of the old lanes built when a train came through, and people who lived high up the mountain needed a quick path to dash down in the morning and not be late. Ahead of me, I could see dozens of tiny bird feet next to her bare ones. A hum of chips and cheeps came from her skirt, a relaxed sound, as they fed on small seeds and bugs in the dirt. She kept walking, up and up, taking the narrow roads—Rose, Edgemont, Tenderfoot—until we reached the dusty mountain fire-trail called Old Railroad Grade. She walked at an even pace and sipped from her paper coffee cup. She never looked back at me, but the birds under her skirt did, so she must have known I was there the whole time, not just at the end, when she stood at a junction, and I crept behind a sawed-down Douglas fir log, and she said,

"You know they are very sensitive. The whole world passes through them each time they sing." Her voice sounded like my grandmother's, as cracked and soft as sturdy shoes. "Inside a towhee's body is the whole town, the whole mountain, tiny and veined. Would you like to see?"

From the dusty junction in the trail where the madrones reached their smooth orange arms down like bare muscles, she looked straight at me. I stood up and brushed my hands over my corduroy pants, trying not to look out of place.

"Yes," I said, and climbed over the log toward her. The sound of white-crowned sparrows came from her mouth. She swallowed more of her coffee. Up close, we were the same height, and she looked young but with hundreds of lines around her eyes. She smelled like the rainstorms that lash you full of a wild desire to trade in your skin for a different one.

I still don't know how it really happened, even all these years later, and I've thought about it every single day.

"Come in," she said, and went first, under the hem and into her own skirt, so that suddenly it was a tent with nobody wearing it, and we were both inside, well beyond its linen bounds, in a field by a dirt trail grown along its sides with elderberry and blackberry and rosehip. All around us, the sparrows and towhees and juncos poked at the earth, scratched up the worms, picked off the last drying berries. All together, their gentle cheeps made a din.

"They are reading the whole ground like you read a book, and the whole sky too. It's full of hawks and airplanes."

Faster than I could believe, and without scattering more than a few of that brown and black river of feathers, she grabbed a junco, squeezed its throat until it was dead, and opened it down the middle with a sharp fingernail.

"Look," she said, and held out her hands where the junco lay, perfectly halved like an open fruit still attached at the rind. Instead of pink lungs I saw tiny, coiled streets and the dark-veined passageways of earth beneath them, where worms and moles move. I saw the seeds of all the brambles and wild grasses, sprouting their different roots, instead of a heart. I saw iridescent plumes of poison from car engines that coiled like arteries, I saw the shadows of bobcats and foxes and weasels, gods on the hunt, where the ribs should have been, where the kidney and gizzards go. I saw the whole mountain, and the town at its base curving in the topographic lines of intestine and liver-vein. Up close, my nose to the wishbone, tipped with blood, I even saw the roof of my own house, where my dad and I would sit and watch the stars.

I felt sick. I felt dizzy, but I didn't want to leave her bird-thick side. She put the body of the junco into her paper coffee cup and secured the plastic lid gently over it. Then she began to tweet and hum.

"Why would you even want to leave here and come into town where people don't like you?" I asked, all at once, because I couldn't think what else to say.

"This is a library and a blueprint," she said, gesturing toward the bush and path and meadow full of ground birds. "I bring them to collect your world, so that when it falls, you will remember why."

Sometimes collapse is slow, until it is upon you, and even then the faces of the dandelions are as yellow and as pure as fallen stars. I never believed the world would fall, like the girl who was also an old woman with birds under her skirts told me.

And yet there came a day a decade later, or more, when I saw very clearly that my dreams didn't fit. That the world was already falling. We ran then, my Ash and I, toward the mountains to the east, where others had run before us, seeking a clarity of being, and of thought. I wished for the maps inside the songbirds, then. I wished for the girl mad as birds to find me then, and show me the way, but she did not.

Our dreams didn't fit at the edges the way the straight highways, the power plants, the oil refineries, cellphone boxes, stories printed in newspapers and in books about square homes and square lives and square green lawns trimmed once a week with hired mowers, the way they fit, corner to corner, a great grid that even the dandelions couldn't break through. It was because of this that we arrived at the place of despair.

And it could only be because of this that he came.

All we had left was our music. I played the fiddle, the way my grandpa taught me, all bow and wail and velvet vibrato. My love, he picked his old guitar and put the crooked black top hat on, because it didn't matter now, now that we had given up, if the world, they told us, had moved beyond top hats, if the world had moved beyond imperfect creatures and un-straightened things. It was winter and the snow came down everywhere around the home we'd made in the dead body of the last old cottonwood in the foothills east of the City. There were no leaves; the branches made bent and antlered songs against the cold winter sky, the moon was too full and the music we played broke our own two hearts all over the ground.

Under the earth, the badgers and the foxes knew how to sleep and hold their own bodies through the cold, how to make a home in the ground and belong there, how to carry on, because no one had ever expected them to learn to button on suits and pat down their wild hair, sit at desks, at screens all blue and white, and carry home neat lines and numbers and rectangles of paper in their pockets. No, they made their beds from such rectangles of paper, bitten to pieces, from soft grass and dead leaves. They dreamed and their dreams fit as the snow fell on their thick coats: red fur, black fur, grey fur, white fur.

But my love and I, we had only our music and the snow and our cold cottonwood home, no other way to make ourselves belong. We had our despair, full and complete, a thing we held between us like a loaf of bread we had no choice but to knead and leaven and bake.

It was then he came, our single dream, through the snow and the bare branches. He came even though there was nowhere for him to fit. He came anyway. He came on perfect wheels of skin and wood and bone; he was a leathery-skinned, ancient, trunked beast, rolling the way no orderly thing, no neat instrument of civilization, should roll. Creature, wagon, tree, with a single candle instead of a horn, to light the way that had been forgotten. His hands were like our hands; they folded a ladder made of his skin down from his wide back, they hustled us up like two frightened owlets who'd lost their mother.

"I like this music," was all he said. He held up a book. "You see, your songs are the ones I have here. It's been a long time, since anyone called." When he spoke to us it was the saddest, sweetest note on my violin; it was my love's guitar and the warmth of his crooked top hat, black as crows; and yet it had also in it the falling snow. Beneath us, the creature's back was warm as any draft horse. We began to play again, and he rolled onward, singing the words in the book he had carried all along, leather-bound just the same as his leathery skin.

Through that whole full moon night in the snow of winter, in the black bare hands of trees, he rolled on wheels of wood and blood and we played on his back. We took the old roads past the culverted riverbed, through the agricultural fields where we were not supposed to tread. We took the roads where people had walked in the times before cars, the ones sheep wore into the meadows, the ones horses trod, even the ones the bears, so long ago, had walked. He could see them, our wagon-beast, our dream, he could find those ancient and hunted paw-ruts. From his leathern back he sang up their ursine song and we learned the tune until our strings bled the blood of ancient bears, drop by drop, onto the snow.

It was then that we saw the people following in our wake. It was then I looked behind and saw them all, a thick road back through the snow, a banner unfurled of thousands—black-haired and brown, red and yellow and silver and white, one blue, some barefoot, tennis-shod, booted, in work clothes, in nightdresses, in winter coats. They were walking to reach him, our last and final dream, our desperate creature born in the dead of winter from all the dreams that wouldn't fit. They were playing a quiet music through the snowfall—sung and slapped, picked on rubber-bands, tapped with the broken parts of cellphones, whistled through metal pipes, hummed on a simple old jaw harp. They carried all the last candles from the pantries, the ones saved for power-outages. They followed the dream of all things living, all things wild, they followed the last paths the bears had once walked toward their dens and favorite acorn groves. In the snow, in the night, our footprints were wagon-wheels of wood and skin and bone. They were tennis shoe and bare foot and fox paw. The ghosts of those ancient bears, they rose, slow and silver and broad, they walked between us.

In the night, he led, we marched.

HARK
HARK THE DOGS DO BARK THE BEGGARS ARE
COMING TO TOWN · SOME IN RAGS
SOME IN JAGS & ONE IN A
VELVET GOWN

The Holy Beggars

2042 CE

WE CAME AT LAST TO THE CITY AND SAW THAT THERE WAS NO MOON, when there had been one only a mile before. It was a clear night, all crisp and star. The moon had been with us on the road, glowing in the dirt, between the bare buckeye branches and the golden globes of their nuts. They hung like planets in a planetarium, the kind you visit in a city, spending your last dime. We stopped at the outskirts, where the meadows turned to abandoned lots and the dogs stalked each other between tires and a rusted car. On the roads that led from the outskirts to the city center we found that the moon was caught inside each streetlamp, like the thousand reflections it leaves on moving water. Each lamp had a refracted piece in it that glowed and shifted like a firefly caught in a Bell jar. Up above, the sky was dark. The city rose like a hill, with sharp edges of roof and tower peak. It glowed silver in its jagged corners with the blood of moons.

"What does it mean, grandmother? Have they taken the moon too?" The twins asked her, our old woman with the ceramic pipe always in her teeth, the one she dredged up from the poisoned riverbed. She was not the familial grandmother to any of us. None of us were related by blood at all, not even the twins who together called themselves Blue. No, we were a found family, pieces picked up along the roadside, under the rose brambles in other people's gardens. The baby who I, too old for such things, nursed—he was one of those left at the back doors of churches by young women. Now that the law has changed, you never know what you might find, peering into cardboard boxes or barrels by the river. It is preferable, though, to the street corner, and the coat-hanger, and the blood all down your thighs. These old breasts of mine, they found the milk still tucked in all my odd corners and stiff bones, and fed him.

"I don't know, my Blue boys," said Grandmother, "I don't know."

It made our hearts all drop, I know it did. I saw it in our faces. Krezki, under his dark hat, always rubbing his fingers on the neck of his fiddle, his long nose moved, his brown eyes wilted. Blue, he went solemn in his two pale faces, the smaller Blue on the shoulders of the bigger Blue. And on her two wheels, St. Rosabelle, our rolling icon, she opened her eyes which were always closed, and began to cry. The coyote who followed us from town to town, eating our scraps, chewing the bones of the skinny rabbits and pigeons we caught and cooked, he began to howl then, as the tears fell from her wood and wimple cheeks. Krezki put his fiddle to his shoulder because he could never resist that howl, and together, coyote and violin, they sang out to the moons all trapped in streetlamp glass.

I rocked the baby at my breast to that old haunted song. St. Rosabelle kept crying, and her wheels creaked. Grandmother pulled a pot from her big pocket and rubbed the spokes and joints with raccoon fat, from the fellow we found last week, road-kill, skull crushed and wet across the ground. The creaking stopped. The moons in the streetlamps flickered and cast the wide silhouettes of raccoons, just for a second, across those city-outskirt lots where we stood in a patch of green weeds. Krezki wailed harder against those old catgut strings with his old horsehair bow. The edges of the city—smokestack, church spire, tall and narrow bank—they shuddered, I saw them do it, I saw them move.

I smoothed out the ragged hem of my velvet dress, the one I wear like a skin. I held the baby on one arm. I began to dance. Stuart, the man who was really a mask and the ash tree the mask was carved from, began to move the woody joints of his knees. That's what got the weeds swaying and the owls to pause above us and almost come down to land: Stuart and his slow tree-branch dance. It made my hair stand up; it made Blue fold up all four hands and stare.

"This is the only and the last place," said St. Rosabelle, and rolled over to the lamppost, where she leaned her wood and wimple head and stared up at the piece of moon. We were so unused to seeing her eyes, they made us uneasy, how dark and how sad they really were. None of us wanted to ask what she had seen, our daughter born of velvet and nave and the longing of holy water.

At the edge of the city, we danced. At the edge of the city, in the dandelions and thistles and nettles right up to our knees, we danced, we sang, the coyote howling and nosing at scraps, his tail a black star in the moonless night.

St. Margaret, Little Owl

2043 – 2135 CE

I HEARD THE SINGING AND THE FIDDLE AT THE EDGE OF MY TOWN like everyone else. I was only a small girl, then, seven years old, but I remember how the strings wailed and shone through the air as the dogs howled in all the backyards.

"Mama, can we go see? Mama can we?" I said this all night long. The music was green as rain-grass in me, and as sweet. I wanted to take it in my teeth and swallow, like any young creature. I thought the moon watched me, big and soft out the window, so close I could see his eyes. The music got louder as the nights passed. Sometimes a tune snuck up the streets at 3 a.m.

We lived simply, then, because of how the economy broke, and then the earthquake, and the big sicknesses brought in often by rats, and the crops failed by dry, dry winters, my mother said, teaching me to use the candles carefully, to cherish their small light when it was dark. Nothing for cars to run on, so they sat in driveways or by curbs, grew orange rust spots. We played in them, imagining travels to far away, with wheels spinning. Every family had a stockpile of weapons somewhere, hidden, Just In Case.

We boiled our water every morning for the day, because it might be toxic otherwise. It felt like a dawn prayer, then: the pot steaming while I sat

impatient, waiting for the bubbles to move faster and faster off the bottom until they rolled.

I remember the sound of the violin above all sounds, like it had the moon and his sad eyes in its belly, on its strings. I waited by the window every night for the music to start, that whole long springtime. My mother didn't like it, the men and women ragged in the empty lots and parks at the outskirts of the city, by the bay, trailing crows and mutts, singing old haunting songs, making everyone feel like crying, making even the stars look unsettled. Besides, she was worried they might have weapons, more than our men did. People will risk a lot, people will be terrible, if they are starving, if they are afraid. That's what she said to me, cleaning the dandelion roots, scolding me at the window for my own longing. She said to me that they would bring disease, like rats, from crawling with scum. She said they would poison us forever.

I already had a fever, at the windowsill, listening to that high and lonesome music, imagining the glowing velvet of their rags.

I remember that time, the music welling up everywhere, like you remember the perfect morning. The yearning can break you open just like the soft sun and its mild breeze. I remember that time all green-glowing at the edges, tinted with a perfection it never quite had, because afterward there was a massacre. Afterward, there was a real sickness, a falling into ruin, faster than any childhood.

When I was small, I knew there had been a Decline, that we were part of it. I knew that adults talked about Before with sadness, because of all the sickness, and all the death, but it felt distant, and my life was simple. We had a garden plot in the square, and two ducks. We lived in an apartment with light switches and wires that never worked. I liked to imagine them up there in the ceiling, tangling through the walls, like roads and highways that led somewhere. Magic roads that could make sparks and light and other things I never could understand but had heard of—music coming out of mesh circles, fans, heat. I liked to read books at night, and did lots of other things in the dark in order to save up my candlestubs. I learned to wash and to make an egg, get dressed, clean my teeth, peel a potato, all in the dark, so my candle, stored in a sock by my bed, could be for reading. A raccoon raised her babies in the ceiling, and pigeons sat on the windowsill and listened to me sing, because I liked to sing versions of the stories I read. I went to school in a cold classroom around the corner. The teacher taught us letters and numbers and the division of one thing into the next, with a strong-smelling red pen on a white board.

I remember the music because it was the last good thing in my life, the last whole thing, green as the hillsides of spring that I could see across the bay, north and east and south, when I stood up on one of the city peaks with my mother, watching fog come in from the ocean.

After three months of that music, that song and rattle and patter of dancing and of laughter, I snuck out the window, down the fire escape four stories, hopping on other families' balconies. I ran to the city-edge, down in a grassy patch between parking lots, beside the old raised up highway and the dirty grey waters of the bay. I followed a fiddle reel and the yap of a coyote for blocks and blocks, like I had the sound in my hands, and it was pulling me. I got mud on my boots, wet and dark, down in the marshy grass. It squelched, and I hid in the shadows, watching a group of seven. They gathered around a bonfire. In it burned brambles and logs, an old chair. Rabbits cooked on spits. Two coyotes napped on golden forepaws, ears twitching. Hands reached out to be warmed. Those seven sang and fiddled and laughed—a man with a black top hat, playing the violin; an old woman gnarled and hunched as a burl of wood, smoking a ceramic pipe, with one hand on the wheels of what looked to me like a painted idol-girl; two boys, twins, hair so dark it was blue, one on the shoulders of the other, beating at drums; a white-haired woman in green velvet who nursed a baby from one wrinkled breast, and sang; an impossibly tall and gangly man, masked, dancing a whirl and dervish, so intensely that the air around him whistled.

They seemed so full of color to me, not just their clothes, but their eyes and their voices, and the way they moved. Like they were incense sticks, glowing and giving off a sweet and heady smoke, the kind to make you uneasy if you aren't used to it. Not the way people were in the apartments, or when you passed them on the street carrying the basket of rutabagas from the farmstands; everyone looked at each other like the other woman might have cheated and grabbed more than her share of the root vegetables, of the tallow for candles, of the matches, which were of a limited supply.

I listened to the man in the black top hat play on the violin the saddest song I'd ever heard until the moon was all the way up. That's when I saw the rest of them; that's when I saw how the music came from every direction along the water's edge, on the old moldering docks and overgrown lawns, up the overpass that no longer held cars, only walkers. Drums played with sticks, dozens of violins, accordions, bamboo flutes, guitars, strange stringed instruments of knobs and sizes I couldn't name, ululating jaw harps, women ringing big fistfuls of bells. They spilled up from the bay in groups that gathered around small fires, like a set of tiny sprawling camps. The music made no sense all together, close up. It was a chaos of sound, different tunes and melodies and keys and cultures from one fire to the next.

From inside the city, the pieces wafted in the air, one tune at a time. Here it was a great net of sound, fishing at the stars, at the city itself. I don't know what for, what great treasure they wanted to catch. But I know they were fishing for something, all gathered, with that woven mat of sound so full of sadness and yearning that all I could do was crouch in the shadows and weep. I did not know the ache of beauty in the world; I did not know the wonder or the umbered eyes of the wild, until that night.

It was as I cried that I saw the creature. Grey skin as taut and thick as leather, and glistening, with a tapered trunk and delicate ears the shape of a deer's. He was bigger than the pick-up trucks you now and then see overturned by a road, grown with blackberries, and he had wheels too, wheels that seemed made of his very skin and bone, five in all, of varying sizes, surrounding his belly and curling tail. He had two hands and eyes as big and dark as nuts. Candles sat on his head like horns. He was a dream thing, trundling through the crowds. People threw milk and dried herbs, vials of wine, at his wheeled feet as he passed, like he was a deity or a moving shrine. A man and a woman sat together on top, she with a fiddle, he with a guitar, and the songs they played rang out like embers cracking, like red velvet shoes dancing, like the black tipped tails of foxes in the snow.

The creature himself whistled through his trunk, a keening sound, high and low toned at once, like two notes being played, one as deep as a lake bottom, the other a thin flash of bird in an open sky. They moved through the camps and crowds and people parted, pressed hands to his wheels like you would to a saint on pilgrimage.

I had not known magic in the world until I saw him, until I came upon their song and dance and open fires burning blue. I wanted to be in it, dancing. I wanted my fingers to press the strings of a violin, move the bow, make those sounds so unafraid. A hand touched my shoulder then, and there was the man in the black top hat, holding a fiddle, grinning beneath a hooked nose.

"A little madam from the city!" he exclaimed, offering me his hand to shake. "I'm Krezki. Welcome! You seem to be the bravest soul around, our first and only guest."

"I'm Margaret. Margaret Cole. I don't mean to intrude—"

"Nonsense, Margaret of the big round eyes, little owl," said Krezki, gesturing with his violin, which swept against the stars. "The entertaining of guests is a high art, a high pleasure, very good for the heart and the digestion too."

I had been hiding behind a leggy pine tree, one of many planted in neat rows in what was once a park by the waterfront. Krezki stroked his long fingers on the bark and grinned as I stared at him and tried to speak.

"Come out from the shadows and join us. I'll show you around." He extended his forearm and helped me up. He brought me to the bonfire I had seen first, where he had been playing, where the old woman nursed, the older woman smoked a pipe, two coyotes napped, a wooden girl on wheels sang hymns under a dark tree.

I can't speak of that evening without crying, now. I can't tell of it like one tells a normal story, with a narrative arc, with a beginning, middle and end, because it filled me to bursting. My nose, my eyes, my fingers, my stomach, my skin, my ears, my young heart. It filled me like music will, all at once, utterly, so no lines can be made between moments, notes, feelings. Nothing in my life has been like it, before or since—the celebration, the carelessness, the joy, the ragged edges that comforted rather than repelled me, the sense of purpose. We are all ragged inside; why not fray out into the world, dressed in red?

I can only tell it in scraps and pieces, a quilt that has come to cover my heart in order for me to continue despite the fact that it is all in ruin, bones and broken refuse, the joy gone from the world.

It was rabbit skin and fat in my teeth, a feral grassy sweet flavor, rough wine and rougher stars, tipping me with dizziness and warmth, the carts of roasted nuts, of porridges and cakes set up on the old roads, making all the painted lines blurry; a boy playing a grand piano on the top of a hillock above the marsh, a piano on wheels as big as a bike's, and pulled by tame deer, how he sat up there amidst the brackish smell of mud and played old songs that waltzed and mourned, how beautiful his face was in the moon, a face I loved that instant and will love until I die; how the woman nursing the babe on her wrinkled breast decked me in velvet ribbons with gold bells at the ends, gave me a ragged silk skirt to twirl and flow over my straight pants, blue as any jay, the ceramic pipe of the old grandmother stuffed and smoking with wild sagebrush and orange poppies, the shapes of two hundred small fires along that cement road and in and out of gray patches, parking lots, so the whole bayfront was a walk in the Milky Way, each bonfire a star, its own shape, fed by its own unique pile of branch, chair-leg, willow shoot, shingle.

I know that Krezki put his violin in my hands and let me play, and though I made only hisses and squawks, it felt like holding my own soul outside my body, letting it speak, cradling it in my arms. No wonder it sounded rusty, never having been aired and held. I know that Krezki said to me, with a wink of his green eye, "we follow the dream of all things living, of all things wild, we are following the paths the bears once walked over the earth, and are calling to them." I didn't understand this, but I knew it was good. I knew that the grey creature was their god and their heart, all in one place, and he was also a dream no man or woman could have made, a dream from the great belly of the ground. When I too got close enough to touch his wheel, I wept because it was warm like an arm or a calf, a living wheel, and then I danced. Someone put a wreath of marshgrass in my hair, fed me the best bits of their soup, wrapped a scarf of bright green wool around my neck, dusted my shoes with pollen and seasalt, with cinnamon and then with rust, until I swear I was gliding, my hands full to weeping, my hair a wild owl of a braid.

I am not sure how I made it home. By then, it was almost dawn. The sun at the edge of the sky, like a skirt lifting, was a silver streak, a pathway, and I was so spun with the life of those people that I could not distinguish between the tar road, the white lines painted up it, the strings of Krezki's fiddle which I could still feel under my hands, and the coming of dawn. I think those two coyotes, and a mutt terrier-hound, led me through the city streets, nipping at my hands, and that there was an owl above.

My mother sat on the steps to our apartment, crying with worry. When she saw me with those dogs, looking flushed, traced with ribbons, marshgrass, rust, pollen, velvets, a bell, mud, she screamed.

*

I have never wanted to know if what followed was because of me. It can't have been, not all of it. But the part that hurts me most, even more than the loss of my own mother, even more than the dead sick bodies of people and dogs in the streets, the buildings crumbled and smoking from earthquakes one after the next, is that it was all somehow linked to that night, the streets of bonfires, the music, the velvet rags of joy. There was only a handful of days between that morning when I returned and my mother screamed, and the morning when the men with machine guns lined up along the road once called Marina and opened fire. I heard it from the window. I heard the music stop suddenly and I ran past my mother who yelled for me to stay; I ran all the way back to that place where the green of music had been ringing. I couldn't get past the men.

They were a barricade of shoulders and the smell of gunpowder. I recognized some of them as the fathers of other children I knew, or grocers, or carpenters. Blood was everywhere, and bodies in pieces I couldn't understand, all over the marsh and grass and the road with the lines painted on it. I did not know how soft and full of blood a human body was until then, nor how hardened the brothers and uncles and handymen of my city, how full of anger and hate. I wish I still did not know. I was so small, just seven; I threw up when I saw it all, when I saw that place I had only just been filled with blood and not roasted nuts, red velvet, fire, song.

I saw their bullets fill up the grey creature on his dreaming wheels. I heard his cry through his trunk, sadder than the moon. I heard one man yell: "demented elephant freak-show!" and I fainted, it all went dark, I wanted to be dead too.

I will never forget him, the trunked and wheeled dream. How when the bullets ripped him, they seemed to light dozens of candle flames in his ribs. How all the hope went out of my body right then, my body far too young to have to give up such a thing.

After, that, everything fell, and fast. The earth moved, again and again, and people became sick. The city smoked, broken apart in pieces, like clouds that one minute are cathedrals with spires, the next all loose and frayed, stones tumbled. Only the churches, the old missions, the temples, still bustled with people. Nothing and nowhere else did.

I don't know how all the pieces fit together; I was too young. I don't know who is to blame exactly, but I do know that the doors of the churches and missions and cathedrals, were polished and open when every other apartment and office building was abandoned or collapsed inward. It was like they had been ready all along, the men who led prayers and confessions and called themselves Fathers, who said that we were the clean of soul, who had survived. That this was Judgment. And the women too, whom we called Sisters, who wore brown habits and white cloth over their hair; they seemed so well prepared, as children and men separated from their families staggered in and began to sob on the stones in the courtyard. Just like I did.

For ten years after the Fall, until I was seventeen I lived in a cloister, in the place we call the Abbey, which was once called Mission Dolores. Tragedy will age you. My hair had strands of white and I was small, not bigger than a girl of ten. Bells rang all day long with the hour, meal-time, prayer time. We dressed in brown robes the Fathers called habits. I was considered musical, because when I arrived, I hummed and hummed all the songs made up from my story-books, and also a single wild tune which I learned from those roving music-makers at the edge of our city, at the corners of the empty lots. I hummed without stopping for days on end and through the nights, until my throat burned and seared. I hummed until the Sisters who watched over my cloister came into my tiny cell and fed me a drink that made me sleep so deep I remember only darkness. I hummed to keep from the totality of panic that winged in my chest.

God, we were told, had chosen us to live. It was the musicians, in velvet rags, with their mutts, who'd brought it—the sickness, the violence, then the fires and the earth moving and all the smoke. They got in the cracks like weeds in sidewalks, like devils. This could have been easy to avoid, we were told; you can't let people like that in. Or dogs. Not raccoons either, with the darkness around their eyes like masks, with their paws too clever and too much like hands. Certain seeds were suspect too—unidentified herbs, exotic fruits. Certainly no mushrooms and their unseemly spores.

I didn't trust the Father and the Sisters from the start. It made my life harder, and it wasn't because I was more clever than the others. I don't mean that. None of us had a place to go; all were afraid, so afraid that at night, silence was so rare as to be alarming. The halls filled, by 3 a.m., with shouts, with children crying, women muttering, my own humming, and later on, the sound of my violin. Sometimes, I even thought I heard the whimpers and wails of ghosts, in a language so different from English I couldn't make out a single familiar word. It was a language like water and the chipping songs of robins. No, I didn't trust them because of what they taught us about the musicians, and what they allowed me to play on the violin, which was the only thing that finally made me stop humming. I knew differently than what they told me. I knew because of that one long night, edged in yellow pollen and the wheeling Lyoobov.

There was a single thing that kept me from jumping off the tallest roof. Only one. It was a room at the back of the cloisters and the man and woman who lived there. It had white-washed walls like every other room. Big wooden beams darkened the ceiling. They were the only couple to have made it through the Fall together. They had a secret that only I knew, and the ceiling of the small room they'd been given to live in was hung with three-dozen bells. I took my morning tea in there with them—some hot mass of boiled roots and herbs from the tired Abbey garden we were all forced to drink daily for our health. The soil everywhere was sour. No one knew if it was poisoned. Nothing grew well that we tried to plant. The trees that grew still on the sidewalks dropped their leaves too early, grew them yellow and curled. But in that small white room, with the woman who called herself Rose and the man who called himself Ash, the tea tasted sweet and round. The sun coming in the windows felt soft on my face and on theirs too. Rose opened a drawer in a beat-up cabinet and took out a sugarcube for us to share on each visit. She had carried them in a tin with her since she was a child, tucked into her belt. When I knew her, she was somewhere near forty. She looked older, and so did he.

It aged them, the massacre down by the bay, more than it ever could have aged me, because they were there. They were in the middle of it. Those men and women, playing fiddles and singing up the blue bonfires, dancing in old costume velvets and doling out roasted hazelnuts and sips of whisky, as the ghosts of bears wandered between—these were their people. Ash whispered to me, tears on his face and his cracked lips, his beard turned all the way grey: "we led them."

He told me that the grey creature, who called himself Lyoobov, was their desperate and wild dream. He was shot right out from under them. When he fell, they were trapped between his wheels, miraculously, as if he had maneuvered his own death so they might live. It was only when the guns stopped, the ground ran dark with blood and overturned nut carts, that they emerged. No one else was left alive. Not a soul. I felt dizzy and sick when they told me this, although I knew it in my heart. I thought of Krezki. Rose still had her violin in hand, two strings broken along with their pegs. Her fist had been clutched so hard around the neck it took weeks to ease the cramp of that shape; her hand is still curved, like she is cupping water.

"We were deranged," Rose told me. "We should have run away, run over the bridge and far north, far inland, run and run and never looked back. But like two ghosts we crept through that place so recently full of song and now full only of bodies torn until they couldn't be recognized, so horrid our minds, I think, shut their own doors and hid. We couldn't leave them all—we who had led them. We did not know how to honor them. We wandered, picking up every last bell, carrying them in a trash bin we found. We cleaned the blood off in the bay. We hid through all the sickness, all the earth-shaking, those months and months of darkness and the moon not moving, trying to tend and to bury, to burn, all of our dead. In secret, so no one would notice. We watched the bridges fall into the water during the earthquakes. We watched how they fell on their knees first, like our Lyoobov, and we cried. By the time the Fathers and the nuns went on the prowl to save all us disheveled survivors, we looked no worse than the rest. No one knew of the bells at all. No one knew the source of the leathery rain-capes we wore, or the single wheel we carried, bone and skin, big as my chest. In the end, you see, we were shattered, and we were afraid. We did not want to be all alone in the world now broken. And now we've found you."

Rose told me this the first time we met, as a wind shook and chimed the bells, as a big moon peered in. I had found them and their secret because one morning I heard a song coming from that little room all the way down the hall. I was ten then. I crept to the door and I smelled something green and rich coming through the cracks. Despite myself, it made me think of that single night I spent in velvet ribbons, full of wild hope. It smelled like new spring green air; it smelled also, impossibly, of rose oil, of woodsmoke and oats cooking. I sniffed at that door crack for months, quietly, at night. One day the door was open and I peeked in. I saw all the bells—silver, gold, grey, black, rust-orange, lichen green—as small as my pinky tip and as big as my head. I saw the wheel, sitting on a single red pillow in the corner. That's when I went in. That's when I went in and I said, straight out, to the worn couple in brown habits who sat by the window, having tea and talking low: "I was there the night before. Krezki fed me rabbit fat and his violin." The woman dropped her tin cup of tea on the ground. It clanked and spilled, blood dark. The man began to weep.

*

One morning, a few months into our acquaintance, Rose and I sat at the window working on the crude table looms that the Sisters give us, as women, to make cloth with. It is a lumpy and misshapen affair, but blankets are blankets. Ash hummed at a song and pretended to be in prayer, in case any Fathers passed in the hall. A little brown bird, plain but glossy, landed by the window. It had been years since I had seen a songbird. She cheeped lightly. Rose stopped her work, flushed, grew teary. I just marveled at her small and sharp beak, the perfect shapes of her feathers. Rose stood and brought her old violin from under the bed. Two-stringed and two-knobbed. D and E. A high and lonesome sound it made, a little out of tune, when she played me a reel, then handed it over. It was like the wind and that small brown bird at the window, cheeping sweet.

"This," she said, "is the sound of our Lyoobov and the snow he came from, all shining and sharp, while we slept in the roots of trees and did not know where to turn. Please, it is time you learned it too. I did not think I would have the energy to try this again, but I find, sweet Margaret, that because of you, I do." Ash touched my long hair like you might a young owl, with tenderness and also care, and Rose placed it in my arms. I cried. I hadn't cried at all, since the day of the blood and the guns. It was like the tears had been put elsewhere. Now, they got all of us wet, and left salt crystals behind. The wind hit all of the bells at once, and we smelled that green blood of springtime and hope, right off the backs of the motley dancers and fire jugglers long dead. It seemed, then, to come right from the belly of the violin.

I played it every day. When I woke up. When I couldn't sleep. To quiet my thoughts, to quiet the world out the window. I played it during mass, to accompany the singing, though I didn't enjoy those songs. But they gave me a reason to always practice. When I played that two-stringed fiddle, I woke cords of green and walked them through the air and into my memory. I wondered, as those cords flew the windows like verdant-feathered owls, where they landed. If there were people out there whom they touched. I was afraid to leave and to search, because I was afraid I'd find no one. I wondered if there was any hope left for us at all. Or if, as he listened, the moon himself wept. I left out a bowl of water there, on the sill, to catch his white face when I played the violin, to see if he cried.

What I found, in the end, was not the moon's weeping, but an owl. Krezki, a lifetime before, had called me Little Owl. I saw that he had known my true name, all along.

I've heard the story told of myself after Margaret, myself as Little Owl Woman. It is not easy, or comfortable, or natural, for an owl to tell her own tale; we don't enjoy the process. It is not a hunt, with a mouse at the other end, but a winding way, with so many twists and turns.

Here is what they have said of me:

It is said that the sound of her wing beats is full of sorrow even as they press the wind and find within it stars. It is said that she is the dream and the grief of a woman some called a saint, a woman who poured water into bowls at night and set them at her windowsill to catch the dark and the moon's face, handsome as a man's. By day, she caught the opening of leaves, the way they grow from nothing into spires of light, a green alchemy.

It is said that an owl came to that bowl of water as she sat in her Cloister at the End of the World. A barn owl, the common kind, who had just eaten a mouse and had blood on the white blade of her beak. That owl landed. She drank delicately through the blade of her blood-streaked beak from that bowl where the moon and the night and the stars rested like fish. It was a cold night, ice on the tiles of the abbey roof, ice on the branches that were still bare of their green, ice on the moon and the stars in her bowl, and the woman who some call a saint looked up as that beak dipped to drink. It felt

like a thorn in her heart, it is said, that beak and those eyes so long and black that she finally found she could see the night for what it truly was—an owl, hunting the shadows of earth for the heartbeats of the furred, all blood and warmth in their nests.

It is said the bowl of water was really her soul. It is said she was a saint because she lived in the abbey in a Cloister at the End of the World, and the Fathers there spoke of God, but it is also said she was a witch, with her heart in a metal bowl of rainwater, reading the night as the city smoked and the gutters cried out poison.

They say that she began to grow feathers from her forearms at that moment, and each one grew sharp and soft as her sorrow under the dark eyes of a barn owl who knew the night and herself more fully than any of us ever know ourselves.

It is said when she became an owl, she left behind two people she loved, a man and a woman, and a beast she had seen killed, who was only bones. But owls, of course, have an eye for bones, a sense for bones, that humans do not. In their chests they have a chamber for them, a place to transmute them, crunched, to bring them up again. It is said that for many years she searched the night-ground not for skunks, not for the blue-glowing bones of voles. No, she searched for the bones of a great wheeled creature whose name was Lyoobov.

They had been scattered all along the edges of the Bay, in the streets of the city fallen to shards, dragged there by dogs. On owl wings she found every last bone. It is said she was only part owl, then, with breasts and a single foot, and her breasts in the dark were cold and hard as moons when she flew. It is said in her eyes the bones shone silver. It is said that a smell of the newest grass, the sound of a violin wailing, lived in the marrow. She flew from one to the next as a pilgrim will do, visiting first one shrine, then another, following a pathway of bones. Except for the vertebrae, the ribs, the finger bones, they were so heavy she flew them one at a time to a special place. She wanted them away from the City that Fell. She wanted them away from the darkness there of which she knew too much. It took her many years to gather all of those bones. While she did, she saw the City scatter into a hundred thousand pieces. She saw the people of the City, and the surrounding towns, gather into Camps scraped together of tarp and tent.

By the time all of those bones were gathered in one place, she would have been a woman of one hundred years, but she was neither woman nor owl, but caught between, and so she did not age.

It is said that in order to bury those bones, she made peace with the moles who saw her ice-sharp beak, her feather white belly, and grew cold with the shadow of what looked to them like their death. She perched and sang to them, something like a hoot and the cry of a violin, until they came, and she told them she would guard their tunnels from All Owls if they would only make her a hole, deep in the earth, for the bones of Lyoobov, the dream of the man and the woman she loved. She asked only that they dig with all their hearts, and then help her to cover the hole up again.

It is said by all the alders, sung by all their yellow catkins and the goldfinches who eat them, that she hung a single bell in the trees above the tunneling moles. She sat in the white branches, ringing her bell, singing poems to the sky in some inbetween tongue, part woman, part barn owl, that sounded quite a lot like a scratchy violin, as they dug.

When it was done, all the bones buried, she covered the fresh ground with the seeds of poppies and lupine, gold grasses, the bodies of voles. She watered him daily. She hooted through the night, and flapped the air with her wings even as she gathered comfrey leaves with her one hand and her talon and laid them across the earth. She hoped they might knit his bones together, like they will flesh wounds.

It was nine years she tended that place, perching up in the branches, ringing her single bell that was orange and heavy with rust. The moles called her goddess, and laid offerings of the deepest soil flecked with dirt against those bones. None of their kind were taken by owls in all the time she lived in the trees near them, roosting in the silvery buckeye one season, the alder the next.

Being only half owl, the other half woman, her hand at last grew restless. She fashioned quills from the feathers she shed, and it is said she wrote strange poems into the branches of one of those trees. No one is quite certain what they said, as she carved in a human tongue and an owl tongue at once, C's and V's and A's interrupted by deep claw marks like runes, and traces of vole and dove bone from her meals. Some say she carved with the quill of her body love poems to a boy playing a piano. Those are the romantics who say such things.

The only one, they say, who every read her etchings in the alder bark as she tended and circled the grave garden of Lyoobov those many years was a young boy lost in the forest for an afternoon, lost from his camp of tarp, of Toolshed, of dancing fool. He told his sister what he read while they were out collecting dry fir branches on the old tar streets of a neighborhood, each fallen house like a dozing horse. She told her friends, and soon all the children of that camp knew, and whispered about it at night, after their Fool had danced and their Master of the Fire had put out the flames.

A tale given to children will change in very odd ways, hooted and hung and feathered. It is said by those little ones of long ago that she wrote down the story of her Lyoobov, her dream, and also the story of All Owls and How They Make the Night, and so it was a broken tangled poem, part diary confessional, part owl-song, ripe with the red hearts of voles and the constellations they make through the dry grass, with some brief mention of how the stars above were themselves voles moving through their kingdoms, ready to be swallowed by that greatest of owls, the Moon.

It is said by the boy in the ripped denim who found it, his sister in her black braids and red sweater who told it, sweeping the tarp-tent for her mother, that the end of the poem was all owl-scratched. That she had become, by the end of those long years, completely a barn owl and no more woman. That it was hard to tell if those marks were full of anguish or the purest joy.

And so she left Lyoobov there, bones tended by the moles, and flew away into the dusk hooting her worship of vole heart and meteor, all owl. She would have stayed there by him, her Lyoobov, until her death, if she had remained in any way a woman and not wholly an owl. But perhaps it was a blessing, an act of grace, to be washed clean by owlness, and only follow the heartbeats of the dark night, no longer the sorrows of the human world.

It is said when she hunts she hunts not for mice but for the night itself, the shadow of the earth and world. It is said she hunts for the night itself, but what is it we hunt through the night, passing between stars and darkness like needles, if not our dreams? What is it we bend over with bowls of stream water tinged with the bark of willow roots, holding them in our single hand, pouring them on the earth where the bones of our heart rest, if not that single and final dream?

Constellation II

There is no
excellent beauty
that hath not
strangeness
in the proportion

The Fools & their Revolt

2191 ~ 2198 CE

•

Wheel

IN THE ALDER WOOD, UP HILL FROM THE CREEKBED, THERE WAS AN open space in the trees and an encampment made of tarp, cob and old canvas tents. In a sunny patch, the women grew carrots and leeks. There, I danced and was called the Fool. They thought I was the product of the nuclear power plant leakage, or pesticide waste, of the Fall, but my mother told me differently, and I knew that she was wise. She told me I was part spider, part wagon, and the rest of me girl. What else can explain the wheels that are my feet and how they collect dew, like spidersilk, at dawn?

There were three dusky-footed woodrat nests next to the Camp. They looked like huts made of twigs. Sometimes I wanted to curl up inside of them and hide. I never felt like rolling for the Camp people on my tender and wheeled feet, but I was always afraid of what they would do to me if I didn't. Some nights, the people were bored, or restless or maybe they felt insecure, with the stars so many above us all. The children sang songs that mocked my curve-backed shape. They called me Quasimodo and they threw old plums. They made jokes, loud enough for me to hear. Sometimes a girl my age with one blind eye stood up for me. Or at least she didn't join in. But she was never brave enough to come talk to me on her own. I could only keep on with my rolling dance. It wasn't so much of a dance, really, just spirals and pirouettes on my wheels. The people liked to stare at something different, something freakish, and forget their own lives in their disgust, their fascination.

I learned to juggle, because that's what they said Fools used to do, in the courts of kings all wrapped in colored velvet. Nobody really knew what they were talking about, but I wasn't in a position to argue. I juggled buckeyes, polished and fallen, or old baseballs. I taught the woodrats to dance on the curve of my back to the strange twanging of the little metal jaw harp my mother gave me when I was small.

It was only because I wanted a friend that I sat at the entrances of their three tall woodrat nests, and I talked. I told them about my mother, who everyone called a gypsy, or a witch, or both words at once, strong and dangerous words that have stayed in our minds, under our tongues, since before the world broke, a hundred thousand telephone wires snipped and dead. The land bucking and leaping like a panicked deer. They called her those things because she lived in an old hay cart pulled by six tule elk, the last to be found anywhere, that was painted purple and yellow. She didn't brush away spiderwebs when they were built between one of her tent poles and the side of the cart, between axle and wheel. If a spider spun a web between one of the wheels and the ground, as they often did on cold October mornings, we would stay, for two days or three weeks, until the web fell in of its own accord, until the lady in the middle had eaten her fill and decided to move on.

There was a tent made all of felt over the bed of the cart. The elk who pulled it were female, so they didn't fight or get their antlers tangled. My mother let them graze often, in the old grassy center divides on the empty freeways, in the pastures that were once for cows. She sold medicines. That's why they called her a witch. Her medicines always worked. She also sold pretty scraps, hoarding them the way woodrats do.

My mother liked pieces of glass jars, the kind once made for preserving blackberries or plums. She liked marbles and coiled bedsprings, coppery pennies which she polished at night when we stopped to make a fire under the stars. She collected tea tins, clear, orange plastic bottles used for pills, beautiful spiraling screws, spoons made from silver, old keys, tin whistles. She never told me exactly where she found that small key-shaped jaw harp, nor how she knew just the way to balance it against the teeth and coax out that strange lonesome twanging. I think it came from the City, and Before, and we didn't talk about it, but I loved the way it made the place between my eyes hum. During the short peaceful time of my childhood, I spent hours with it while the elk grazed and my mother gathered elderberries.

Above all things, my mother loved to find the rectangular "brains," as she called them, from inside old computers and phones. They shone metallic, with a thousand strange lines and squares and geometric patterns, some ridged and some flat, like maps to the underworld. She kept all these things in neat baskets inside our moving home, and showed them to customers who came for elderberry syrup, for lemon balm and poppy petal tea, tinctures of coastal sage for menstrual cramps, datura and dark speckled mushrooms for visions.

I was only nine when she died. I should be forthright, I said to the woodrats. I was only nine when she was killed. I was only nine when they surrounded our little cart, when they shot the elk for food and took us here, to burn her the way witches have always burned, they said. I alone was proof of her dark power, they said, with my wheels for feet, the way I rolled, my body more curved than a raccoon's. The people of the Camp burned her. They made me watch the fire take my mother piece by piece, screams that licked up toward the sky with the flames. Only I, listening to my mother scream, sick all the way through my bones and out my wheeled feet, could hear that in her screams she was also singing her curse.

Afterward, they buried her black bones in a hole, and they had a feast. They ate the body of one of our elk. I was sick and the tears made my body sting with salt. They tied me up to keep me from running, though I never would have got far on my slow and glistening wheels.

So you see, I told the woodrats, sitting at the messy entrances of their dens, I don't do this because I want to. I do this because I am afraid they will burn me too, if I try to escape. I am not as brave as my mother. I do not want to die. And where would I roll to? I asked them. I know what people do now, to us, to the ones who are strange. It is worse, sometimes, than burning.

That was when they started to come out, to run up my arms and sleep on the hunched plateau of my back—when I told them the truth, that she was killed. I think they liked the vibrating little metal jaw harp too, which I played almost more than I spoke, making sounds like stars calling out to each other. I taught them to stand up and balance my mother's golden marbles on their heads. I taught them to twirl, and to somersault. I don't know why they listened to me. Maybe it was the folded-up scraps of aluminum I left at their twiggy entrances, like offerings. I folded them as I talked, into tiny crisp birds, balloons, stars. When I came back, they were always gone. Maybe it was just that I sat so often, talking to them like you do to friends. Or maybe it was my wheels, spoked and flesh and spidersilk.

I say they are spidersilk, though of course I don't remember my own conception. I never knew my father. But my mother told me, when I was young and barely understood, that my father was a man and also a spider, and I believed her. I still believe her. What else is there to do? It was on early, dark nights that she would tell me about him, when she was quieter than usual and had a sad, sorry look at the edges of her lips, at the corners of her dark eyes, tucked into the coils of her brown braids. She'd have already lit a fire from dry oak twigs in the narrow woodstove tucked into our tent. The elk would be unhitched and grazing. They never ran away. I don't know why. Maybe because my mother loved them, and they knew it. She'd put me on her lap and let me have a sip of her brandy.

"It was a day just like this one," she would begin, gesturing to the early dusk, the chill, the leaves the color of fire, and falling. She said a spider had made a web attached to the left back wheel of the cart one cold November morning. She saw it while she was out feeding the elk a treat of wild oat and honey cakes. Dew hung on all the threads. The spider in the middle was as orange as the leaves, legs striped just like stockings. His body as round as the moon, save one single taper, where the thread came out. My mother was mesmerized. She sat down in the wet grass, a big flat meadow right next to the old airport runway, cracked with weeds, and watched him weave. She imagined what it would be like to have silk thread coming right out of her own body, to build her own home in the air. She longed for that. She watched him for days, even when he sat motionless in the center of the web for hours.

Then, one morning a week later, when she ran out early under a wet blue dawn, the spider was gone and the web ripped to shreds by raindrops. She was so sad, the rest of the day, she told me she couldn't eat. She closed up the small back door of the haycart, kept her vials of herb on the shelves, and did not answer to any knocking.

Night came clear, with armloads of stars. Finally, my mother opened the felt flap door to look up at those stars, which reminded her of dew on spidersilk. A man was sitting right outside, in the mud, smoking a long, orange pipe and holding a book in two hands, reading it in the dark. At first my mother said she only stared—he wore clothes made of velvet, the orange of sunsets after storms and persimmons about to fall with ripeness from the branch. Black and brown lines spiraled across his velvet coat in the finest needlework. It was only slowly that she saw how he smoked his pipe with one hand, held and read a battered paperback with two others, reclined in the grass with still two more palms, and had three resting quietly in his lap. It felt like dizziness at first, all those arms. She counted them, and when she got to eight, he looked up at her from his book, removed the orange pipe from his teeth, which she saw were quite sharp, and said, "I've been knocking all day now."

My mother told me she let him in, and they made love on her narrow bed of felt and fur. She was held in eight arms instead of two, and the whole cart turned warm and orange as an ember around them. Even though I was too young to understand, she would say to me, brushing my hair with her hands and blushing, "to make love with an eight-armed man, my wheeled child, that is beyond all the pleasures of the world." She never told me more than that, only how, in the morning, she woke to find him nowhere, and the inside of her haycart-tent covered, from side to side, with spiderwebs round and pinwheeled. They clung to the glass jars and plastic bottles, to candlesticks and tabletops, to each ceiling corner.

"It was the spider who first invented the wheel," my mother would say, at the end of the story, "not us, not man."

The woodrats listened to my talking every day, and then they came out, every dusk, walking on silver feet. I loved their silk ears and the fur on their tails. Three of them came normally, now and then four. They climbed my arms, up the slope of my back. I gave them each a small and shining object from my pocket—silver key, paper clip, copper-colored battery. It was these objects they danced with, on the raccoon hump of my back, as I rolled on my two flesh and spidersilk wheels in slow spirals and figure-eights. They stood on their hands and looped their tails, balanced their treasures on their heads, swayed to the sound of the jaw harp.

It took me a year to stop watching the faces of the people in the camp I called mine. I pretended, when I was there pirouetting by the fire pit, doing my job as their Fool, that they were not real, that each cackle and hiss, each leer, each expression of disgust and release, was mechanical, like the bodies of the computers my mother collected. Then, I only felt afraid, but not hateful, and I could go to sleep in this body they called deformed, even loving my wheels, because the people were machines in my mind, and knew nothing of what it meant to be truly alive, to feel the dirt spinning under your soles.

I danced and made music as their Fool for three years, until I was twelve. I danced every night before they went to bed. They said I was their nightmare-catcher, and they would sleep sweetly after watching me, after listening to that eerie twanging. The rest of the day, I kept out of sight in the alder wood, learning the different personalities of the orange-bellied newts who walked the creek, the woodrats in the nests, eating my pail of scraps from last night's dinner. I never tried to run, because there were guards posted along the edges of the wood, where it met the open meadows, day and night. It was dangerous, that world; people from outside wanted what you had inside, even your piles of trash. That's what they made us think.

The morning I turned twelve, I woke up by the woodrat nests with pain in my abdomen, in the bowl of my hips. It was dull and cramping. I thought of the women who slipped out of their encampments to see my mother for herbs to ease their bleeding and their cramps. I knew what it meant, when a woman begins to bleed. I sat up, afraid, and went to gather the plants my mother used—wild blackberry leaves, the bark of the yellow willow. All morning, I waited for the first blood to come. I drank my tea, and the pain eased. When I finally felt something wet on my thigh, I didn't want to look. I didn't want it to be true—me, alone, a Fool who was also a Woman. With my fingers I felt along the inside of my leg, and found fine threads there against my skin instead of blood. I looked down. Spidersilk lined my leg, moving briskly out of me in delicate tendrils. I only stared, and gathered it up around my hands as it came.

I had two fistfuls, soft and coiled, before I realized that the feeling in my chest, around my mouth, was joy. The part of me—a small seed as heavy and dark as iron—that had believed them when they said I was made from the poison of power plant flumes, that my mother was a lying witch and nobody is fathered by a spider, that part of me dissolved. All that was left in its place was a dense ball of spidersilk, my inheritance.

The black phoebes darted from the alder branches, chasing insects that hovered over the creek, and I played with those wheels of web around my fists. The woodrats helped me carry strands up into the pale branches. They scuttled up the trunks and tied the webs there with gray paws. I found that I could climb them. I could roll up on two strands with my wheels, each piece a track like the railroad ties you see, covered now in weeds, dark orange cuts and lines through old city edges. The webs fit into the grooves of my feet, around the fleshy spokes. They held my weight, sideways in the air, ascending. My hunched back, hands dangling toward the ground, my gait always cumbersome because of that arch in my spine, it became perfect. I could pull myself along on the tracks of two strands, feet rolling, hands climbing. My back became the curving horizon, planetary and smooth, that turned my whole body into a spoked wheel and a spider at once.

I thought of my father, all dressed in orange velvet, with eight orange sleeves. I thought of the web my mother watched for eight days on the wheel of our cart, while the elk ate down the nettle stalks rampant between the decayed bodies of airplanes, collapsed at the edges of the tarmacs like giant dragonflies. I knew then, climbing my own silk through the trees, testing my speed and my strength, scaring the gray squirrels right off their branches, that my mother, whatever her flaws, was no liar.

They must have come looking for me that evening, to be their Fool, when I didn't roll down quietly through the alders to the center of the camp, past the wooden planter boxes of leek and carrot. They must have come to the place I always slept, next to the woodrat nests, and found only the thick web I left behind, between each twiggy lodge. I wove and rolled my way out on wheels and webs. The woodrats ran ahead, across the open meadow, past the sentinels. They carried strands in their teeth, up into the next copse of trees on the hill, bishop pines. At dusk, as the stars pushed out their silver mouths and breathed upon us, I wheeled on two tracks of spidersilk above the guards, above the encampment, above the trees, and free.

The three woodrats slept in my pockets as we rolled through the treetops and spooked the ravens out of their nests. I didn't know how many miles I'd gone from that place where I was the Fool, the nightmare-catcher, the daughter of the witch whose bones lay black under the ground, before I stopped, and made myself a proper canopy web. They hunted, for a while. I watched from above, curled in the old nests of great-horned owls. Their dogs sniffed the ground for me and howled at the treetops. But no one thought to look up, to strain their eyes for a gleam of spidersilk between the sun-green leaves.

And so I was gone from them. I lived in the canopy, in hammocks of silk, travelling my own train tracks through air. I ate the fruits of the trees—black walnuts, peppernuts, plums, apples, nuthatch eggs—and was satisfied. My only friends were the woodrats. Down below, things continued as they were—the camps, scared at their edges, the Fools dancing by fires, the old cars, airplanes, hotels, caving in with weeds and the weight of passing clouds. One day, I knew would drop down on a line. I would be brave, I would gather with me all the Fools who were lonesome, who carried the nightmares of our kind on their twisted shoulders. One day, I would be brave for my mother. I would show them the spider-strands of my body, the freedom of wheels, the kinship of woodrats. But back then, I was only a girl, and afraid, alone with the dawn birds, the dusk stars, the newborn leaves.

Martin & the Thumb of St. Francis

NO ONE FISHED ANYMORE, NOT AFTER THE SALMON RAN FULL OF poison. A small girl with a milky blue eye was the only one left alive the morning after the coho were roasted and eaten along their autumn spawning run. I grew up in the Buckeye Knot, which was closest to that Camp, where everyone lay dead in their beds. The Master of my Camp ordered us to set fire to the tarps and tents and bodies. It was in an alder wood, damp by the creek, so only the encampment burned, along with several woodrat lodges. No one could sleep for days, watching that smoke, how it moved against the treetops and the sky in piscine shapes.

A fish ban was enacted. No stories, no songs, no mention of names—coho, Chinook, steelhead, bluegill, perch. Certainly no fishing, no touching those bodies which were thick with the remnant poisons of other times, when everything toxic had been poured into the water and forgotten.

This was the only explanation anyone could come up with—the poison from Before, it was circling back from whirlpools out in the ocean. The fish carried it in their fat, in their livers and eggs. Only the blind-eyed girl didn't fit. She complicated the story. She had eaten the fish, too.

In the Buckeye Knot, pale-trunked and green, people muttered in their canvas shelters, their wood, car-door and tarp houses, kept bright and neat despite the constant fall of leaves, about witches. They whispered about the Fool with wheels for feet, and how she had disappeared only a few weeks before the poisoning. They whispered about the burning, and the black bones, and sipped at old spice jars full of the rough brandy made up north, from the half-wrecked vineyards.

I don't know about the other fathers, but I know that mine kept telling fish-tales to me all the same. He told them quietly, at night, so no one would hear. We climbed up a big buckeye together, one with dozens of thick branches grown like a mat, and my father made up constellations in the shape of fish. Salmon were our favorite to find out of stars, whole migrations of them.

"Whenever we ban things," whispered my father, "we come to hate them. We don't mind killing them for the sake of it, for fun. The whole world has been poisoned; fish are only messengers."

The autumn after the deadly spawn, the coho came again. Every last one was netted up and killed. The bodies made a pink and silver pile that stank, and was burned. That year, my mother died.

For years afterward, the coho were slaughtered until there were none left at all, and I dreamed about fish. Little ones no bigger than slips of light, big ones like my father said lived in the ocean, as big as the trucks I sometimes saw, growing into the roadsides with their coronas of teasel and broom. I dreamed of climbing inside those big fish. In my dreams, they showed me the bottom of the ocean: pale blue light, the thick salt and murk, metal hulls of steam ships.

CONSTELLATION II

When I was nine, and good enough with a knife, my father let me carve a small rod out of a buckeye twig, even though all fishing equipment had been buried in a box in a hole and covered, like a grave. I strung it with gut and a hook made of the big rosethorns people from the Camps near the old towns traded, stripped from bushes in wild front gardens.

That winter, I sat with my short fishing pole at the openings of gopher holes. I fed the thorn-hook and line into a hole, and waited. I was four when fishing was banned, when the salmon and trout were killed, and then stopped spawning altogether. I couldn't really remember what it was like to sit with a real pole by the green water of a lake, line dangling through the currents, waiting for a bite. But I thought about it all the time; the string, with you at one end and the fish at the other. How still you sat, just waiting for the line to go taut, that pathway to the underwater, to the dark and wet places where fish live, breathing in the water.

It was a game—the buckeye twig, the twine and thorn, dipped into badger tunnels or excavated mole hills. I liked to be alone, and quiet. I was covered in so many freckles that the other children called me Mudface-Martin. I was glad they couldn't see the freckles on my chest, on my thighs and upper arms—I was speckled everywhere. Like stars, said my father, and called me Starboy. We hunted for fish on my arms too, making up new brown-dotted constellations.

"I'm full of quiet," I told my father. "If I'm not quiet, I think mom is still here." It was an infection from a cut in her foot that killed her, where she stepped on an old and rusty nail, but when I was a boy, I always thought she had gone wherever the salmon had gone. She was with them where they vanished, and if I fished, she might be found, resting with them. When I was quiet, I felt full of hope; I could push all of her living movement and laughter out of my mind, her jokes and her fast way of talking, how many curls she had, half matted into auburn tails. How they always bounced and fell from their braids and knots.

Stillness, and the magic of fish; I filled up my head with them the winter I was nine. My father let me sneak off with my buckeye twig and thorn because I always came back glowing, as if I'd actually caught something. Really, I just sat in the tall grass, pole in hand, by the tunnel of some creature, and dreamed. Dreamed I was underground riding the backs of fish, underwater against silver scales, thrashing upstream with the coho, and my mom was there too, shrieking with joy.

Seeing her that way didn't both me. It was how they'd burned her body that bothered me—how all her red curls and loud voice just went away in the flames, on the pyre, and when it was over she was ashes, which the Master of Fires swept into a big glass jar, the kind salvaged from empty houses. He placed the jar full of gray ash on the shelf in the Dead Room, next to all the other jars of people from the Buckeye Knot who had died.

She was just like a tree that had burned, or the white ash in a firepit. Irrevocably gone: the evidence of her absence in those labeled and shelved jars, in that damp clay-smelling room of cob.

I'd heard stories of other Camps that buried their dead in the ground. At least then, I thought to myself one morning, wiggling my fishing line gently in the hole of a gopher as the January sun began to dry the dew from the grass, you don't have to see what happens to the body. You can imagine them down there, speaking with roots and stones.

Looking back on that morning, I recognize the signs—something wild had been in the air, even before dawn. I couldn't sleep the night before. Instead, I took my old felt blanket outside to look at the stars. Though father and I came nightly to arrange them, I couldn't recognize any as I sat, wrapped in the itch of wool, peering up. A dizziness, queer and lost, shook me, and I went in again and lay awake, watching shadows made by the moon move across the floor of their circular home. They touched the wooden platform floor, the canvas and felt walls. Father slept heavily, and once said, "Mary", in that voice I remembered from when mother was alive, the sweet voice my father would call her with.

It made me cry, and then I thought of the Fool dancing by the firepit the night before, like he did every night, with his seven hares on leashes, flipping their ears at his handless command. I remembered the look on the Fool's face—blank except for his eyes, which pooled and snapped with more grief than I could fathom, until I realized that I carried the same grief when I thought of my mother—that the Fool and I might be similar. I wondered what made that man a Fool, and not myself or my father. It couldn't only be because he had been born handless; it couldn't be that a Devil took his hands, like people said. What Devil could command seven gentle, gold-coated hares to dance and flare their black tails, eyes wild? There was nothing evil in that, not as far as I was concerned.

All of these thoughts sat with me that January morning as I fished in a gopher hole. They were shifting, subversive, uneasy thoughts that tipped and tilted through my heart like glass marbles. A twist of wool from my cap began to itch, so I set down my fishing rod for a moment to scratch and straighten. The buckeye pole lurched across the ground, then, pulled by its suddenly taut string. I snatched it seconds before it vanished entirely into the hole in the ground.

A great weight tugged from below. Not a stone or a root, but a moving weight that lurched and wiggled. Gently, with sweating hands, I pulled at the buckeye rod. I didn't want to startle the Thing, or hurt it. I imagined that I'd hooked a badger by accident, or maybe an exceptionally strong mole. I figured I'd ease it aboveground, unhook the barb, and place it back in the hole. It might be nice to touch a mole's dark fur. My mother had worn moleskin gloves in the winters—ones she had killed and skinned, tanned and sewn, herself. The people used to seek her out for all their sewing jobs. I loved to hold her hand in winter, when it was covered in moleskin, soft and rich.

Preoccupied with the memory of mole-soft hands, I didn't notice at first the smooth and scaled nose that emerged from the hole, breaking free clods of soil. When I did see it, all at once, I yelped and dropped the pole and pulled the whole body up with my bare hands, gingerly, like a newborn wet with birth.

The fish was half as big as me, and heavy. Slick as clay and polished wood. It kept coming and coming, breaking a bigger hole in the ground, tail long and curved. I collapsed beside it where it lay, twitching its tail in the grass. The fish was hinged, carved, polished. It looked like a dark dream, like starlight and freckles and all the constellations my father and I had made.

"Hello," I said finally, unsure. The fish bucked and writhed. The hinge at its tail, brass and bright, flickered in the sun. I wanted to reach out my hands and hold the fish, stroke its scales, which looked at once alive and carved on by a knife. I wondered suddenly if I'd killed it, pulling it out of the ground, where it must have been at home, breathing through the dirt like other fish breathe through water. I didn't want it to be dead, but I also didn't want to put it back underground, where I couldn't watch it: finned, scaled, tapered as a leaf.

The whole meadow, swaying with purple needlegrass and an old hiking path through it, snapped then, like a linen in the wind. The fish's mouth burst open. An old man, brown-bearded, in brown robes, as small as a gopher, wriggled out of those jaws like a breech-birth, feet first.

"Been looking for a way up for ages," said the small man. Tousle-haired, like he had been through a storm. He patted the nose of the fish, prone, beside him.

"Is it a real fish, sir?" It just came out; I couldn't help myself, though I knew it might be rude, though I knew that a man the size of a gopher emerging from the dirt was more sensational, even, than a three-foot fish, polished and hinged. But it was the way my imagination suddenly touched the world under my hands, like the two were connected by a ribbon of living muscle, that filled me up, that fixed my young green eyes on the fish and less on the miraculously small man, brown and neat as a monk.

"Real? What an odd child you are. Do you see it thrashing in the grass, seeking dirt to breathe through, poor chit? Do un-real things thrash for air?" The small man pushed his beard aside and began gathering together a high mound of dirt. His hands small as blackberries moved fast, nails square and worn as a gardener's. "What the hell are you doing, just staring? My fish will die. Come help, your hands will do the job much quicker." The man gestured toward the mound of dirt he was piling up from all around him—soil from mole hill, gopher tunnel, grass root. "It's like an oxygen mask, a water bubble. We can bury her gills in this."

"But sir, it's hinged, it's made of wood and clay."

"Indeed," replied the little robed man, and pointed again to the mound. I crouched and scooped up handfuls of dirt. Within a matter of minutes, we had created a loose and loamy pile. We didn't speak as we scraped and sifted. Only the scrub jays in the trees overhead quipped and hawed and darted on bright blue wings. We patted and mounded the dirt up around the fish's gills. She lay quiet at last, breathing gently.

"My fish," said the man, folding his knotty hands with the grace of a monk and sitting down with his back to those fine brown scales. "To begin with, my fish is a she. Not an it. Egg-full and lovely as bark, when she's in her element. I made her myself." He smiled with pride and took a paper, folded and old, from his pocket. "My blueprints," he said, and held them out, tiny as mushroom gills, to me. "I keep them on me always, like other people might keep a Bible."

"So she isn't a *real* fish then, the kind you eat? You know, that used to come up these creeks and spawn?" The blueprints were like moth wings in my hand.

"My child, she is fully a *real* fish. What you refer to is a *flesh* fish. She is part so, Chinook, half-eaten by a grizzly and left to rot under a blue oak, buried up to her gills in humus after only a single winter."

"But sir, there are no grizzlies. They are myths, before the Gold-Time, my father told me. That was hundreds of years ago."

"And I am hundreds of years old, of course. Would I lie? Really, you are troubled by the oddest things. How old do you think are the roots and bones under the soil? Several centuries, to say the least." The man snatched the blueprints back and folded them in his pocket, looking stern.

"Of course," I said, and stared more closely at the fish, and then at her maker, that buckeye-smooth man, ruckled and grinning again.

"It was once thought rude to be so inquisitive, you know. I could start prying about all of your freckles, and it might make you squirm, too."

"But I just came that way. It's not like I painted them on."

"True, my child. And neither she nor I came as you see us. No, we began as bone and dirt instead of egg and blood. Backwards creatures we are. You are right to pry. I, like her, began as a nub of bone. A saint's relic, no less. His thumb, brought all the way from Spain and placed in one of those adobe Missions, where they had iron bells and matches between grizzlies and bulls, the missions full of native people, dressed in wool, digging the rows for potatoes, warping and weaving the rough-shod looms. You look at me like I'm lying, like I'm full of horseshit, or maybe like you look at any old man, spinning yarns before you like dark and needled webs."

"No," I said. "It's only..." I stopped and looked down at my freckled hands. I thought of my father, and the stories he liked to tell between the stars. Thought of my mother, her glass jar of ashes, her moleskin gloves, her boots which were her grandmothers' from the Time It Fell. Thought of the Fool and his dancing hares, whose chests were sometimes painted green with a watery dye from nettles and rusty nails; how he told tales of Mission Bells like they were planets from a different galaxy, alien and dreamed. "It's only that it's usually in scraps and tatters," I continued. "All the stories. Like a quilt but full of so many holes you mostly just see the Camp in the Buckeye Knot through it, made out of tarps and felts and tires, and not so much the fabrics pieced together. But you know the whole thing. You have the whole blanket on you!" I felt happier than I had anytime since before my mother died. It was like being the only one to discover a persimmon tree bearing orange fruit in the corner of an old backyard, each one an ember of sweetness and crunch; so good you could forget the whole world except for it, and the smell of rain, and the ravens chortling above.

"I don't have the whole blanket on by any means, only a humble cloak of moleskin. I've been underground, my boy, with my fish, for so many decades. I only know, from that other world, what I saw when I sat, a thumb-relic, on red velvet, under glass. And the glass began to fog and crack after the Mission closed down. I was pillaged from it, along with the velvet, stuffed in the pocket of some gold-rush gambler, but I fell out that same day, when his horse tripped on the road and threw him. It didn't take long for the rain and dirt to cover me, just like my fish—a bone, mired in the dirt and sinking, mole trod, laced with mycelia. Everything else I know begins underground."

"But whose thumb? Which one of the saints were you, sir, or are?"

"Saint Francis of Assisi, of course, namesake of that great city risen and fell. The man who held passerines on his thumbs, you know, and spoke with the black-cuffed bears, fish and honey-breathed. You may call me Frances, if you like. And your name, lad?"

"Oh," I said. "Martin."

"Ah yes, like the old Hungarian saint, horse-man and warrior, so generous with his cloak."

"I don't know about him, only the purple martins that build muddy nests."

"Indeed," said Frances, looking unconcerned. "Well in any case, I don't think I myself was much of a Christian, though they called me one later. I was more a bird-lover. I remember mostly only what a thumb knows—the feet of a sparrow, the foreheads of bears, mint and wild thyme leaves, crushed for tea, rough boots, the hardest and the softest parts of women. You see, my thumbs at least, those ages ago, they were full of un-Christian pleasures."

Frances went quiet, then. He touched the belly of his fish gently, straightened the buttons down the front of his moleskin habit, and pulled a pipe out of his pocket. It was bright white, carved from a shrew bone.

"You don't look much like a thumb to me," I said shyly, wanting Frances to continue.

"No indeed," said the small man, packing a crush of leaf into his pipe bowl and lighting it with a scrap of ember from his pocket.

"You carry fire too?" I leaned close to see.

"Secret," said Frances. He kept his pocket closed. "We've been deep under, my fish and I. To the places where the plates meet and sometimes mate. Magma." He took a long puff. I stared.

"I was buried, you see, in the den of a pregnant broad-footed mole. By some fortunate accident of weather and traffic. She dug her nest right where I lay, a cold bone, and used me as a brace, like any root, when she pushed her babies out into the dark. They scrambled all over me as they grew, dripping sweet mole-milk from their snouts and whiskers, right onto my joint. She crooned mole-songs into the dark to them, songs that were sharp and full of stars and the rings of worms. I began to change, to grow, just like her babies. The bone I was before, that ancient thumb, began to splinter and reform, like some strange caterpillar in his cocoon. I grew in her presence, and she became frightened of me as my feet and arms and hands emerged. She took her little ones and fled. I, alone in the mole-den, was a small and naked man, brown as a nut. Not a boy, but an old man, you see. The thumb, after all, was from such a man, already worn.

"For a while, I followed in the wake of that mole family, eating worms and the occasional bulb. I came to appreciate cultivated fields, where I might come across a potato, even a carrot—sweet as heaven itself. I made myself these robes you see, from the skins of the dead moles one now and then finds, expired in their perfect tunnels. They keep one warm as can be, in the underground. After some time, though I couldn't possibly say how long, I came across her." Frances patted the side of his fish. Her tail moved gently on its brass hinge. "She was only Chinook bones then, supple and almost transparent with time. Her tail had been snapped by grizzly teeth, neat as can be. I made her a new skin, new muscles and scales, from the wet clays and the root-wood of oaks. I polished her with my own hands, and gave her scales drawn by mycorhizzae. I found that hinge just laying near the surface of the ground, beside the cement-pour of some foundation. Quite clever, I thought. I named her Lily.

"My dreams kept me from sleeping much down there. That and the perpetual darkness. I dreamed of Long Before, when I was a thumb bone resting on red velvet, the Mission walls ringing. Boring dreams, really, but they don't leave me be. And I dream her dreams too, my underworld Chinook, my Lily, since I am in her day and night, with my back to her old bones." The little man sighed and took a pull at his pipe.

"It is her dreams that really exhaust me. They are great rivers of salmon, every time, in the thick of the upriver spawn, the jump and thrash of silver bodies in a great Delta of slick water and reeds. They are pushing against the current, up rivers, in the shade of cottonwoods and willows. It is overwhelming, Martin, each dream is river rapids and the paws of grizzlies, fishing. This immense pull inside toward the spawning ground of her birth, like a scream of longing. The bear ate her—a big sow with golden ears and a black snout—right before she could lay her eggs, and dance about a big male, and settle down to die. So every night, her bones dream. I've made eggs for her to carry, little wild onion bulbs dyed red with minerals, bright red like her eggs would have been, like a thousand hearts. That way she feels she has a purpose, my Lily." His voice was full of love and of sadness. I loved the fish right then and there, and Frances too, my very own miracle.

"Why did you want to come up, then, when you had so many things to do down there, swimming about?"

"The solitude, my boy, the solitude. My Lily, after all, can't talk back to me, not the way you can. I am tired of being alone in the dark, plagued by dreams and the sound of my own voice."

"But what about her? Aren't you all she's got? What will she do, up here?"

"Maybe," Frances said, eyes long and quiet, staring through the meadow to the Buckeye Knot, all pleached and pale trunks, "I will make her wings, and gills to breathe the air."

"I'll help you!" I jumped to my feet, full of simple conviction. My knees and calves wobbled, numb from sitting so long on them as I listened. Above, the sun had passed through afternoon and was sinking into dusk. "We can find you old pieces of tin, or thin poles, maybe kites? My father is handy. Maybe the Camp will lend some tools, like the Scissors." I felt hot in my stomach, on my cheeks, like I'd seen the magma-embers in the heart of the ground with the man who had once been the thumb-bone of St. Francis of Assisi, and had swallowed them whole.

"Are these good people here, at your Camp?" Frances stood and brushed the dirt from his robe, which reached right to his bare brown feet. There were dark hairs growing all over his toes, more fur than human. He combed his fingers in his beard, shook out knots and a shard of snail shell, iridescent inside.

It was a question I didn't know how to answer back then—good or bad? This was all of my world. People were the people of the Buckeye Knot. People were my father, my dead mother, the other children who called me Mudface for my fields of freckles, because they were normal and I was odd.

"Oh yes," I replied. "They will want to hear your stories. The Master of the Shed—that's what we call our leader or chief or whatever, because he has the lock and key to the Shed, where all the tools are for making things, ones people have dug out of piles and ruins—he will help you. The Master of the Shed is powerful, you know."

"No, I do not," said Frances. "But I suppose your hook caught my fish for a reason, like the finger of a God, answering my longing, and there is only one choice."

Night gathered cold and clear in the tips of the Douglas fir trees up the western ridge. The dusk sky was as blue and pale and thick as the seedpods of eucalyptus trees, the kinds that lined old residential streets, and as spiced.

I used my coat to hold the fish, so her gills could be kept covered in dirt. I carried her like it was a sling, gentle. Frances fit in the bowl of my hat, so I carried the jacket with Lily in one hand, the cap open in my other where the small man sat, cross-legged, serene as a monk.

At the fire pit, the Fool was combing the fur of his hares and getting ready to dance. My father ate soup from a chipped clay bowl and talked with the seamstress, the new one who mended people's boots and coats with fine gut string. She was laughing, sharp-toothed, black-haired, with a dark mole right between her eyes. There were two-dozen more, hard men with their hard children, hands smudged with fire ash. Their wives sat separate, together with their daughters, some blue eyed like the feathers of kingfishers, some dark with necks like loons, the one girl with her milky blind eye, which had witnessed everyone die around her. The people sat, eating soup from chipped bowls, tied together by their fear, each ring of it like a disturbance in water; the Buckeye Knot held us in like the outermost ring, locked from the world and all the ways it had fallen.

The Master of the Shed sat in a rocking chair. It was the only chair. The rest of us sat on logs. He brought it out of the toolshed every night to sit on as dinner was made on the fire by women, as the Fool danced. He ate, and watched, running a hand often through his gray hair, kept short and close with the Scissors.

I could wait no longer. I set down my bowl and stepped into the firelight. "I have a miracle!" I exclaimed. I held up the fish and my cap. Frances looked at me, alarmed. My father glanced up from his soup, away from the laughing teeth of the new seamstress. He stared at the small man, the big wooden fish, me, and his eyes went full of anguish. I felt cold, then. The people sat on their logs, the Master of the Shed on his rocking chair; they all set down their chipped soup bowls and swallowed down the last of the roots in their mouths.

"Got a dead fish, Mudface? Call that a miracle?" It was the boy who always called me Mudface, bigger than me and flaxen, with strong hands that could break thick pieces of wood. "Trying to poison us?"

"She is a wooden fish, and no poison at all. Her name is Lily," Frances said, and stood up in my hand. A woman screamed and put her palm over her daughter's eyes.

"Yes," I continued, not knowing what else to do. "This small fellow made her. They've been under the ground, he's as old as the Missions, you know! Isn't that a miracle?" But I felt sick suddenly, at all the faces and the firelight, the way the buckeye trees around them cast rippling shadows like a cage, the way the Fool had made himself busy with the ears of his hares, and wouldn't look up.

"What things of witches have you got, boy, and where did you dig them up?" The Master of the Shed rose from his rocking chair. It creaked behind him, moving. Frances ran then, out of the cap and up to my shoulder. "What the hell were you thinking?" he hissed, but I could only shake my head in horror. I felt like crying.

"They are special, Master," I managed. "They have stories from long ago, and from the underground. Don't you want to hear them? They are Things We Don't Know."

My father had tears on his cheeks now, watching me stand there, watching how I didn't take a step back, only held firm to the fish and the perfect old man, small as a mole.

"And what Things should we know, that we don't already?" The Master of the Shed was a tall man, and close up, he smelled like the metal of spades, axes, scissors, rust. I took the fish out of my jacket, defiant. I held her up, glistening in the firelight. Her hinged tail flicked.

"Look, she is beautiful. She is perfect. Not evil. She was here with the grizzlies." She thrashed for the air of soil. "I'd like to help the small man build wings for her." Someone laughed. The Master of the Shed, his two hands faster than flames, grabbed the fish and the little man, and held them high.

"This looks like witchery to me. Maybe same as those poison coho. Vessels of danger, not like us." The Master of the Shed tightened his hands.

"Stop!" I yelled.

The Master of the Shed kneed me in the stomach then, and threw Lily and her maker straight into the fire. There was a single scream from the small man, like a branch snapping. The fish lay still.

When I came to, stomach hollow with pain, the fire was dead, only smoke. I crawled upright, saw the tiny bones of the man, the bigger bones of the fish, and began to cry. They were big sobs that filled my stomach further with pain.

"Shh," said a voice from the dark. I went quiet.

The Fool stepped out of the buckeye shadows. Seven hares followed near his ankles, silver in the night, ears trembling and erect.

"I put the fire out, when everyone went. So it wouldn't burn as hot. To save their bones. Bones can always be planted, you know." He stepped closer and held out his handless arm to help me up. "He said for everyone to leave you here, all night, while they burned. Your father tried to help you but the Master got out his shovels, and swung them, and your dad, he ran with the rest." Close up, I saw the Fool was a young man, no lines on his cheeks. He only moved like an old one, stiff, like sadness spread through all his joints.

"Thank you," I said. I took the handless arm and stood. The stumps were round and smooth. The moon through the buckeye branches shone white and thin as a rib-bone. A new noise rustled and cracked its footsteps through the humus. We froze. My father emerged, holding a backpack stuffed full. He took me up in his arms and kissed me on both cheeks.

"You found your fish, my boy, you found it. But you have to leave here, quiet as a mouse. It won't be safe at all, not after that." I saw tears on his face, and the solidness of it all hit me then. Salt gathered and fell on my cheeks too.

"No," whispered the Fool. "Don't cry. My hares are good luck you know, and can find their way in any dark, through any maze." He picked one up into his arms, a female with teats, leggy and soft. She kicked out her back legs once, then calmly sniffed at the air near me.

"But there are guards at the edges. I'll never make it," I said, scrubbing back tears with my wool coat.

"I saw the hole you pulled them from," my father said. "I measured it, I shone a light. It is deep and just wide enough for you. Grab all the bones from the fire, and take them down and through. They will lead you through, it is the way of such things." He handed me the backpack. All three of us, with the seven hares sniffing at them, leaned over the ashes.

"Get every bone," hissed the Fool, and sifted out a rib. Scapula, vertebrae, femur and dorsal fin and skull, we picked each out, toe bone and fin, charred and damp. We placed them in the front pouch of the backpack. The moon moved over our heads as we sifted. Soft hare-noses breathed at my feet. Buckeye leaves, a wet humus under them, smelled of rot and smoke, smells that filled me with sadness.

Only once, my father laid his arm across my shoulders, held my freckled cheek. "The stars match you," he said. "It should not be this way. A father should not stay behind, but he must, or you will be found. For I cannot fit with you in that hole. It should not be this way," he finished, though I didn't know what other way it could have been, even as the Fool, looking up at those words, shook. Hare-quick, hare-soft, his eyes dark.

My father left me with a kiss to the span of freckles on my cheek and the backpack heavy with the ash-wet bones, a stolen knife, wool sweater, a brace of dried persimmons, my mother's moleskin gloves, a big deerfat candle, almonds. Special things, all. The Fool who would not stay behind; who said his hares were luck, his shoulders narrow; who took nothing with him but those seven jackrabbits, dancing, was at my side. Together the Fool and I crawled into the hole where a fish and a little saint had been dredged up that morning, a lifetime ago. Behind us, my father held up a burning lantern and could not get a word out, only watched until we had vanished into the ground.

From above, it probably seemed that the hole in the earth had eaten us, a swallow of dirt. A wriggle and squeeze, and then it widened. The hares ran ahead, sniffing.

"How do you know it comes up again?" I said to the Fool, afraid in all the close dark.

"I know nothing. It's the hares who do. I only listen."

Ahead of us, the seven jackrabbits moved, quick and sure as stars. Their black tails began to glow then, just like embers. The Fool looked at me, and grinned.

Ffion

1650–2198 CE

LIGHT CAME PALE GREEN AS LICHENS THROUGH MY GLASS. I COULD still smell the sloes and brambleberries of melomels once fermented in it, but they were so faint they might only have been my dreams. The human smell lingered: nail clippings, a scrap of brown hair, a scab. I had pushed the pieces themselves out the bottleneck centuries before, but the scent crept near, still pressing itself to the glass. It was hard to shake, the smell of humankind. We cling to the world like ticks. Only way to get us off is to wrench and turn counterclockwise, until our teeth loose their grip in the great skin of things.

Whatever the words of the charm, it worked. I was a witch caught in a glass jug, and the light came in like the green of new vetch. A letter stuffed, nose first, into a bottle made for distilling fruits, sent out onto the waves, all white-lipped and roaring. It was the binding of hair and nail and blood, an old earthen animal magic, that kept me there so long. That sort of thing always works. I couldn't get out.

A family does not like to leave behind their witch bottle, their demons all caught in a single place. It made them feel safer when I was there, stoppered in with the nail clippings, even though they couldn't see me. I was buried under a hearthstone in southern Wales, near the sea, for two centuries.

Toward the end, I could hear the picks and blasts, the ponies dying from dark and strain and soot. The coal nuggets moaned their chants of dead sun and the rotten leaves of eons past, when trees were soft-barked and birds and fish were the only creatures with bones.

I wasn't guilty of anything too serious, to get caught in that bottle. I'm a simple witch, always was. I lived down by the sea in a house made of worn stones. I cooked kelps and crabs for my luncheon. I was called Ffion. I brewed small vials of sea otter heart-blood for love charms, salmon skins for wisdom, the feet of pelicans for grace. I was a very tidy business-woman, really, keeping neat logs of my sales, my recipes, my stocks of pelican and kelp and rare driftwoods which I carved into small dolls. I did keep a hare as a pet, which gave the townsfolk some unease, though in truth she was a rabbit, an angora, expensive thing. A sailor, anchored near my beach and eager for a woman's arms, had left her as a gift for me, from the burnished ports of Istanbul. She slept always beside me, needy creature, and I brushed her daily to gather the soft, gently crimped fibers of her fur. I spun and knit all manner of neck cowls and gloves with that wool, softer and warmer than any round shaft of sun. Good for the wet and salt-streaked sea air.

It is true, I also spun her chestnut wool into cords, dunked in sea water and singed with smudge bundles of dry saltgrass, and journeyed upon them from house to house, as on a tight-rope, knotted between chimney pipes. I could make my bones pelican-light, and waltz. There is a certain power tucked in rabbits, moon-changing and wise.

They had a right to call me a witch, for I did deal in vials of herb; I did tend the bodies of dead seals, all speckled when they washed to shore; I did now and then cause a toothache, a broken leg, intestinal cramps, bright rashes, but only to those who deserved them. Only once did I cause a man to die, and it was for the sake of his small daughter, to whom he did unspeakable things. Him, I choked and hung with a cable of angora wool, left him dangling from rafters.

It wasn't easy to make myself light as pelican bones, ready my rabbit-fur roads, and breach the stone walls around the town of Tenby, or Dinbych-y-pysgod, as we said in our tongue. It made my joints ache and my wrists bruise for weeks. Those stones were laid to keep invaders out, to protect the furs, the oils, the orange-crates, the velvets—all the goods of trade.

Of course, those stones could not keep out the rats, who carried the Black Plague in their dark and patchy fur. More than half the town died, then. The bells of the chapel rang out each day, until every last man in the church was dead too, and no one had the courage to enter the wooden doors and carry on that ringing. I couldn't save a soul. My medicines were too humble. Pigs ran wild in abandoned houses, rooting through vegetable gardens and closets alike.

Naturally, those left alive blamed me, since I had survived, and saved no one. The next time I walked my ropes of angora, to make a man go bald who had skinned a fox out by the high road and left his body to rot, he was ready with the green glass bottle full of rusty nails, his hair, a scrape of skin, a puddle of urine. Wedged it right in the hearth. In I went, with the sound of an orange being squeezed from its peel. Already pelican-light, I crumpled like a linen, then shook myself, and could find no way out.

I remained under that hearth for two hundred years. More, maybe, I can't be sure. The only benefit of being stuck in a bottle is that I, like a jam or a pickle, was preserved, suspended in time, ageless. Eventually I was dug out and wrapped in a spruce-wood trunk with the bed-sheets and a rosary—dreadful sweet-smelling thing—and put on the ship with the rest of the family, grandchildren or great-great-grand children of the man I tried to curse. They were heading for the place called New South Wales, where the eucalyptus grew with smooth bark and hooked green leaves.

I was only a short time there, and all the while, it seemed the eucalyptus trees were crying, filling up the air with their spice. The family to whom my bottle belonged, they barely settled down in a cabin made all of eucalyptus wood when I was snatched up again and placed on another ship, this time heading for California, for the city of San Francisco, grown elegant on gold and entrepreneurs.

We never arrived. The ship went down. I became a letter in a bottle, bobbing on the sea, waiting to be read. Sounds got caught inside. They bounced off the glass for weeks, sometimes an entire winter. The sounds on the ocean were all new. Before, the chunks of coal, mined out with picks and ponies and carts, they had screamed for darkness, for the weight of the earth above them. To be free-standing, and then lit on fire; this was terror, and they had songs for it, those compressed pieces of darkness and of time. The songs echoed in my bottle where I lay, curled beneath the hearthstone; they came up mole tunnels and through the foundation, travelling all that way in the veins of the underground. I have sharp ears. A witch must have. Then it was the eucalyptus, their green and spire eulogies, as they were cut and milled, smoothed, planed, processed for oil and fiber, making the houses in which people lived. Their songs caught in my jar like the banshee cries of my homeland, shrill; they splintered around me like shards of light.

But the sounds of the ocean, these were the most beautiful and also the most difficult to bear. For centuries after the ship tipped, cracked, filled with water, I heard the sea and her lament. I bobbed and drifted. I saw the gray whales hunted for the oil in their bodies, the elephant seals for the same; I saw the sea otters shaken and razed from kelp beds for their furs; I heard the murres and cormorants shrieking out overhead for their stolen eggs, taken by the barrel-load. I heard the chinook and the coho salmon, all silver and black and red, dwindle. Ships fueled with steam came, then went, and ones filled with petrol, big as cities, replaced them. Plumes of poison now and then streaked the water. And I saw the whirlpools of plastic begin, big enough for a thousand pelicans to stand on, every color in the world you can imagine, but lodging in throats or around necks.

Floating on the ocean, I saw cities collapsed like churchstones. I watched scraps drifting overboard on the sea. Time and ruin, like two black cormorants, airing their waxen wings. A cello, buoyant and warped. A city made all of silver thread and urchin-spines: the ghost of San Francisco.

I heard the ocean, finally, grow quiet. That was the worst thing. I felt ill in my glass bottle for days, wishing for a sound, any lament. I wanted desperately to reach land, but the currents wouldn't let me. Nothing is worse than silence where there once was a hum of chaos, lovely and green: seal, plankton, kelp, coral, shark, tide and salt. A sheen of petrol, iridescent as any dragonfly, clung to the surfaces of waves. I saw the blueprints of cities in it, odd-shaped to my eyes. They were unlike any I had ever seen, those centuries ago on the south coast of Wales. Then, I knew only London, and it was a spired net of stone and wood, a dense and winding grid, all tapering tower and dome and gabled rooftop. The blueprints I saw on the sea were strict rectangles and lines, drawn up with straight edges, everywhere an angle. In the oil-sheen, these cities perpetually shuddered and split apart from within. They crumpled and smoked and all the edges went soft. I watched them as the tides pulled me.

It was another century, at least, that I floated in the quiet. It must have had something to do with my strange crumpled weight in the bottle—I never thought it took a thing so long to fall out of a ship and meet land. It could have been two centuries more, even, after I began to see those cities of petrol, after the ocean went silent, only one whale to be seen in every twenty-five years, and then none at all, that I was swallowed down, glass and all, by a large elephant seal.

She didn't bite, just swallowed, so I passed through the red soft muscles and passages of her digestion. The size of me killed her, a glass barricade. I was impermeable. As she died around me, keening into the salt, and a thick darkness descended where once there had been blood moving in veins, her flesh above me filled with stars. It was like watching constellations appear after the sun has set, one by one and then all at once. What's more, these were stars I knew, mirrored in her body: Cygnus, the Pleiades, Orion, Ursa Major, Cassiopeia, Scorpio. They speckled her stomach lining and her ribs like nubs of candle-light, eons away. In the middle of all those death stars, I saw one constellation I could not recognize. It looked like Cetus, the great whale, only inside was a mad clustering of stars shaped like those horrid sharp cities, fallen to splinters.

I knew then, all at once, that this was the last whale. There are things a witch comes to know, quickly, in her blood, particularly a witch raised on seaside tides, bound to bob the Pacific for centuries. This was the last whale, and all the creatures of all the oceans knew it in the fibers of their beings. They grieved. This was the last one, a humble gray whale, not the biggest or the fattest, but hardy. He had taken all the cities and their rifting poison, their new-fangled bomb-lances of every conceivable making, right into his body like a brand, and died of it. All the poison of my kind: it went first into the seas, the Place it Began. Then it seeped outward and made its way toward the land.

I cried then. The tears slipped against the glass. I had not cried yet in my cage, for all those centuries. I had kept calm and quiet, venturing far away each day into my mind to stop my self from madness. But I cried then, in the dark of a seal belly, over the runes, star-sharp, of the Last Whale.

Night came. I knew it without any way to see. I would know it without eyes. Night, the shadow of earth, fallen. Stars opened up their eyes, crystalline and hot. It's my ears, my hands, that know, catching at the sound of dark carried on owl wings or the moon. A silken feeling along the palms, soft, a slight pressure, as a handshake. I'm not called a witch for no reason, after all. A regular woman would not have been caught in a glass bottle to begin with. She wouldn't fit, for one thing. It would have no power to pull her inside. And if anyone tried to force her, well—it would break all the bones in her body, quick as twigs.

Night, it came rustling overhead, it came sweeping at my palms, and the elephant seal, she stopped, suddenly, her drifting. I felt resistance against her, the slight buffet of tide, the hiss of pebbles. Land. Through the dark, the waves pushed her further and further up the beach, rolling.

By dawn, gulls were picking at her belly. Then a coyote. She chewed at the abdomen in big toothy bites to get at the heart, the liver. She peeled back that skin tougher than any leather with patience, using her mouth as precisely as a seamstress's scissors. Eventually, I saw her black nose, the spikes and tapers of her quick whiskers. When she had eaten her fill, closing up that hunger which made her single-minded, she sensed me there. She nosed at the bottle, pushed partly through the purple-white stomach sac, made an opening. She whined and fixed her golden eyes right on my face.

Animals can always see where humans cannot. No one ever noticed me in there, you see, curled up like a fetus in my green dress, nettle-dyed, with my auburn hair still in its coiled braids, just the same as the morning I left the house by the sea, tiptoed my way on sea-witched strings of angora right over the walls of that port town, Dinbych-y-pysgod, and into the bottle of the fox-killing man. It is extraordinary, all the things that people don't see. It is a matter of honed senses, I suppose, of the reliability of scent, light, rustle. Animals use these signals, these signs. People tell themselves stories of what they are meant to see, of what is expected, of how the world works, and so they see their own stories, and not the world. Not the rage of a fox, dead and skinned in the road, rotting. Not the grief of whales as one by one they died until they were gone. Not me, curled in a bottle made of green glass, trying to be patient, watching it all, holding back my own tears.

The coyote nosed and pawed at my bottle until she had partially dislodged it from the elephant seal's stomach. I could see better then, though the fluids and fibers of that pinniped streaked the glass. Waves, foam-fringed and rough, broke in gusts on the sand. The cliffs, a crumbling ocher stone, rose up steep behind me. It was like my home, my shack on the strand facing into the Atlantic those ages past, only bigger, wilder. No people, only the changes made by tide and wind, only the twisted pine trees up the lips of rock.

There was a silence in the air, under the waves falling in thunder, under the spray and the breeze. A stillness. The world had changed so much and so quickly while I lay curled in my bottle. I was part of that change only in fragments, a feeling and a sound coming now and then through the bottle-neck, standing in for the things themselves: war, power-plants, coal rising up from the smokestacks, cell-towers, oil rigs leaking, cement over the prairies, the marshes, the old graves. The wind carries sounds off the skin of the world, town and child and hearth, and drops some of its load on the ocean. I heard enough, bobbing for centuries, preserved like a lemon in brine, to grieve. No witch, I'm sure, has lived as long as I, nursed on salt water and suspended in glass. No witch, I'm sure, has listened to the death cries of the last whale, has seen the cities fall inside the grime and petroleum floating for eternity in the waves, spelling out stories. No witch has had to endure so much, and I was never even ambitious.

I didn't desire adventure, only my seaside home, the secrets that the kelp leaked out on the shore. I only wanted to brew up vials, to right the small and everyday wrongs, walking the tight-rope cables of my angora fur: men who wantonly killed foxes or beat their wives, women who stomped the herbs in the lanes and weren't sorry, who thought only of their own beauty. I think, as I floated, that the world became full of more wrongs, big ones and everyday ones, than I could ever have faced. I'm glad I only drifted, glass-bound, and caught it in small pieces.

By the time the woman with birds in her skirts found me there on the beach amidst that dead elephant seal, it was all over. The lines made by my own species had been broken. The wind and wild and wave had come in again, even if the wind still held the poisons from cities, the waves all the plastic bits of decades, the sadness of all that melted ice, even if the wild creatures, the old forests, the streambeds and the marshes, were battered and diminished. They still moved in again: dandelion, coyote, barn swallow, spider. They grew in all the breaks. It is amazing, truly, how fast a rubber tire may become overgrown with vetch, and how soon a mother skunk will raise her babies in it.

She was the first person I had seen in centuries, a woman in tattered skirts, long ones that almost trailed in the sand. At her bare feet, a thousand other feet moved. Tiny ones, belonging to ground-feeding birds. I noticed this first, because my vantage was low to the ground. She walked like a young woman, with a slight slouch, head cocked and glancing all around, feet and hips loose. She prodded at piles of kelp, at weathered plastic bottles and tarps, as if looking for something. When she got close, I saw that lines spread across her skin, thick as maps, delicate, more like tattoos than wrinkles. Old age sat regally in her black eyes like a crow, preening and wise.

Those eyes found me. They saw me right through the glass. She smiled, sat down on a driftwood log beside me, and a flood of ground birds seeped from her skirts, covering the seal carcass with small forked feet, poking it for maggots. I will never be able to describe the relief of her eyes—human eyes that met and saw mine, that rested and recognized me. I had looked no one of my own kind in the eye for a dozen lifespans. It felt like a home, her gaze touching my gaze.

A brown bird, simple, all dun, jumped up to the rim of my glass and dipped her beak in. I reached up to touch it, like a handshake, and then the beach and cliffs, bird and woman, spun around me. I reached and touched that smoothed beak and found that I was free.

There seemed to be too little of me to fill myself, a jar of sea-water poured into a copper tub. My bones echoed. The bird, called a towhee, sat on my shoulder and her beak against my neck made noises like bells do—wood to metal shell, hollow. I sat down, body echoing with old sorrows that now had room to move.

"You, I think, have seen quite a lot," said the woman with birds in her skirts eventually. She pulled a gold flask, small as one of her sparrows, from a pocket. "What is your name? I have been waiting so long for someone to talk to," she continued, and took a sip from the flask, then passed it to me. I drank. It was something bright green and strong, like all the herbs from all the mountains I could see rising green and brown in the distance had been distilled together. It burned my chest. I laughed then, and smoothed my hands over my coiled hair. The sensations of hair on palm, of liquor in chest, were as strong as sustenance to my just-unfolded body. I started to feel less hollow.

"I have not spoken," I said, and it came out in roughened slivers, "in four hundred years. I have hummed, but not spoken. My name is Ffion."

"Yes." She paused. "I have been called Iris," she said. She grabbed a robin in her fist, broke his neck clean, and opened his abdomen with a sharp nail. "Here, you can see, It Fell. How I knew you were coming, all along. Like a thread thrown across half the planet, stitching." Inside the liver and the gizzard, the pink pulsing lungs and the elegant coils of gut, I saw what I had seen in oil spills on the surface of the sea, the cities loosening like clouds do in the sky. Land breaking from itself in big quakes.

Small as a pinhead in the center of it all, amidst cities and innards, I saw my own hut of stone and slate. I saw a brown and silken rabbit, and in her silk, in her dark ears and the loft of her fur, I saw myself floating in a green bottle on a green sea, and I saw that town of so long ago, Dinbych-y-pysgod, overgrown with willow shoots and wildflowers. No one left; only barn swallows and a group of wild boars. Then I saw, amidst the willow shoots and tumbled walls, amidst the entrails of that robin's belly and the fur of my rabbit, a woman climb up, balance, pace the edge of the stones. She was black as coal from head to toe, crying out to the sky. I heard that soot-dark lady cry like she was a voice inside my own head. She cried out for the dark of the ground, for the dense pack of carbon and sun and long-dead ferns, compressed in their natural deaths.

"I can never go back!" she screamed. I saw she was transparent, the dark spirit of the coal. "You dig it up, you can never put it back away." She carried a bag on her back. It was lumpy and full of rough chunks of coal. She dug holes for them, one by one, patted earth on top. "I will never go back," she whispered, and dug another hole, crying.

Iris took the bird away then, closed up his stomach, slipped his damp body into the pocket of her ragged dress. She plucked the heart out first and ate it, like a raspberry. My cheeks, I found, were wet.

"Come with me," she said. "It's time for us to begin. There must always be three of us, you know."

The brown, black, red, dun, yellow and white birds rushed back beneath her dress. The elephant seal carcass was picked clean of insects. The glass bottle that had been my home lay in pieces in the sand. I put one in my pocket. I did not know why she had waited for me to begin, nor what it was that needed beginning, nor this business of three. It seemed to me that beginnings were over for our kind, that all there was left to do was end.

"No," Iris said to me, without turning back. A chickadee sat on her shoulder, chipping. "We can't help it, but begin, and begin, and begin."

I walked behind her for miles, through the sandy beach, up a streambed in the yellow branches of willows. Our words came out like rare stones picked up on the shore, at random, savored. She never told me where we were going, only grinned and handed me hazelnuts from a pocket, like they were an answer. The stream passed a meadow, and we walked on deer trails in tall grass, brushing ticks from our legs. I saw rusted cars beside their wheels, a collection of wood and blue tarp and metal pipes, smoking in the trees.

"Walk like you are not here," she said to me when we passed. "Witches are treated the same as they ever were. Worse."

The ladder made of spider silk was thick but so translucent that I would have missed it entirely, if not for the sun's angle through the fir trees and the five house finches who burst out from beneath Iris's skirts and landed smugly on the rungs. She hiked up her dress, then, and began to climb. I followed, thinking of rabbit-hair ropes, wondering where this all would lead.

We climbed the ladder high into the canopy of a fir forest, past ravens' nests and slumbering raccoons, up into the peaks where the wind moved every spire in delicate circles and the hawks landed to look out over the land.

At the very top, the ladder's edges fanned out, part of a woven mat of threads, like the silk canopy stretched over a tent at the fair. A silvery rat with white paws bounded along fine tracks of web to sniff us, followed by two more. They wore golden rings on their tails, and the insides of their ears were dabbed blue. Here and there across the canopy of spider silk—woven with a warp and weft like a woman does, not a spiral, like a spider does—burrows went into the canopies of branches, making snug chambers. Double-banded pathways pinwheeled off in every direction over the treetops; an intersection of highways. Scraps of pretty things hung from twigs and needles: barn owl feathers, bright fabrics, wheels worn of all but the metal, antlers, horns, plastic beads, weathered bottles.

I smiled at these, and then she appeared, a girl with wheels for feet, dewy and supple as the webs around us. Her back was hunched all the way over, so her hands trailed near the ground. She moved easily across the webs, wheels hooking and rolling, hands grasping and propelling her forward. I saw terror in her eyes, an animal fear. A silvery rat nestled in her shoulder blades, dozing.

"You are the child of a witch," said Iris, hoisting herself free of the ladder and onto the web itself. She swayed with the topography of feathers beneath her skirts. The girl looked panicked, and also relieved, even as she rolled backward at the word.

"She was burned." Her voice had brambles in it, and buds.

"I am a witch," I said, wanting to soothe her, seeing now this tattered trine we made.

"Some things may only be begun by our kind," said Iris, and the birds murmured at her ankles.

"I'm no witch," whispered the girl, "only a runaway Fool. A deformed one too."

Iris smiled and gestured around her at the webs, now aglow with morning. "If this is not magic, well."

"It is only what all spiders can do."

"Exactly," I said, because I found her beautiful, and sad, and so alone. "Magic is only that which all other creatures know, or have inside their leaves, and we've forgotten. Or don't care to remember."

The girl stared at me, as did the rat on her back.

"What is it you want begun?" She cupped and un-cupped her hands.

"I want to let it in again, at last, the magic. What form it takes is not up to us, but opening the door is," said Iris. "The Fools, you are the ones who carry it. The only ones left. Your mother's kind were all burnt." A handful of towhees wriggled free of her skirt and flew up to her shoulders.

All the woodrats climbed to rest on the girl's back, then. I saw a smile, sad and sweet, touch her mouth as she watched the towhees, and peered at that big and ragged skirt. "You can call me Wheel," she said.

"It has been so long," whispered Iris. "I can't even tell you how long. A body can only bear so much of this sorrow." I saw tears speckle and then coat her face, like stars which have waited patiently to come out.

I tell you this as an old woman. I have aged, out of the glass, like any mortal girl, gone from twenty-four to seventy with the turning of planets and stars. There is much more to this story, much in between, but I tell you this part because it is about endings, and then beginnings, and the tight ropes we walk between. I tell you this part because she was right; we will always be like thistle-burrs stuck to the ankles of does, finding every last patch in which to re-seed, to remake our world, until there are none of us left at all.

I tell you this because it is true; we did, in the end, prop open a small and knotty door.

What went out, and came back through, well, that is not for me to say.

What I must say may sound less important than doorways propped open, but may indeed by the most important thing of all. I do have a sense for such matters, being a witch, and having floated in a glass bottle for an age on the dying sea.

It is a secret, well kept, that Wheel herself, like all women, was a door. She was with child when we first came to her in her webbed treetop home. She gave birth to a baby girl some five months later, in the heart of a buckeye, and named the child Anja. People thought her immaculately born, of the buckeye. Wheel let them say so. She knew what suspicion had done to her own mother. It took her longer than the rest to trust that the world had changed.

Anja, Anja. There are already many tales about little Anja. Long after I am dead, Anja's story will be alive, and perhaps truer yet. I have loved her well, and yet I fear I hardly know her at all.

It has been many years since I saw Anja or her Martin, many years since they went east. Sometimes memory can be like a glass bottle, keeping someone always the same inside.

In my memory Anja is always a careless fifteen. The sun is rising and she is dancing with the boughs of a firtop in the morning wind, one palmed branch in each hand. She turns, feeling me approach through the webs, and the sun illuminates her face and the spiked halo of her hair. I see she has tears on her cheeks. I am startled. Anja never cries.

"Aunt," she says to me. She has always called me thus. "Why do little ones have to die?" She crouches down and shows me a tiny tree vole nest tucked into the lower branches of the fir, near where the webs of her mother Wheel are woven fast. In that cup of moss and bark and fur are five tiny vole babies, all dead. They have perfect, minute paws. Their eyes are squeezed shut.

"An owl must have taken their mother," I tell her, surprised she is made so sad by this. Many creatures must die, so that others may live. I wonder now if she is dancing to push away her sadness. Anja is not often sad; she has no reason to be. Her life is full, and safe, and gentle. When the feeling comes on her, she does not quite know what to do.

Later, I see her carry the nest down the web-ropes to the earth, where she digs a hole with her fingers and buries them all together, like a bulb. She is weeping again, crooning over their small paws. She does not know I see her, but I see many things I never say. She does not mention it again, and later, over dinner, she laughs often, showing her teeth to her own sadness.

I am an old woman and a witch still, and this is the memory in me that will not rest. Anja and the morning sun and the little nest. I cannot tell you why, because I do not know. Only sometimes I dream of her in the snow, in the mountains somewhere, and in place of her belly is a nest of baby voles shining like stars waiting to be born.

Constellation III

Wild Folk

2288 CE

Bells, Perches & Boots

Bells: Yet I do ring, I chime, brass and wood. They toll, my bells, tallow-bright as summer, crying out our hearts. They sing and clatter, tarnish and swell.

Perches: It was marsh-dawn and no sorrow. I sat by the saltgrass, sewing hawk-thongs. There were scars like rings on my every finger, delicate, falcon-made.

Boots: But I am not only my soles. I walk with my brothers, tangled in our tinkering, quilted in our wares. We are welded like a wheel, stitched like a shoe, together in the dust of roads: each man, he seeks his own particular grail. Bell, boot, a bird that perches and that hunts.

No storytellers worth their salt will tell a tale only of themselves. We three once walked the length and breadth of this land, leaving stories everywhere we went like seeds. It was our good work, our pilgrim's penance. Here is the story of a telling, and of a tale.

No one knew where we had come from, how far or how long we had been walking, when we arrived at the edge of the ocean called the Pacific and unloaded our blue and gold cart in the center of a meadow-bluff of purple needlegrass and iris, just at the edge of a village. The one of us called Perches stuck his tongue out to taste the air, while the one called Boots sifted a handful of dirt and the one called Bells closed his eyes, plugged his nose, and listened. We reached our conclusion in unison—"it is good"—and got to building a fire. Boots hung a cast iron pot over the flames. In it cooked a quail and wild onion bulbs. Perches set loose the four tawny Jersey cows who pulled the cart, and they began to graze.

The children of that village by the meadow-bluff of iris bulb and seed were the first to investigate. They came in pants of deerskin and nettle, here and there a special patch cut in the shape of a star, clamshell, wheel, from an old velvet or corduroy. They hung at the edges of the field, daring each other to creep one step closer, and one more, until a boy named Henrymoss had touched the blue and gold stripes on our cart, bringing back news to the others that it was real, sturdy and wooden, that it smelled like oiled leather and rust, with the faint sweetness of blackberries, that inside he had seen piles of bells, neat shelves full of boots, a bucket full of sticks, branches, wires, each with a leather tag and letters etched on it. That around the corner four cows were grazing, and their eyes were dark brown.

"We are connoisseurs," one of our voices called out to the children where they huddled behind the cart, whispering. "We are pilgrims." The voice had a lilt and a roughness that made several children, the younger ones, run off to the pine trees, to the huts where their mothers sat gossiping and spinning nettle fibers while sipping shots of dark mead.

Bells hung along the edge of our cart roof, and a pair of fine calf-skin boots was affixed to the front, above the door, like a figurehead. The boots were dyed red, laced with grommets, and embroidered with small crosses like stars. Ontop of the boots perched a kestrel, smaller than the shoes, cream and charcoal and pink-orange feathered, with the most beautiful, kohl-dark eyes the children had ever seen. She, good lass, made a shrill call when she saw them.

Henrymoss, having been the one to touch the cart, felt he should maintain his reputation, particularly because the girl Jay, hair tousled and so black it seemed blue, was there with the others, watching and twisting her fingers in the tufts of her dark feathered hair. We could see he wanted to run when he heard the kestrel but instead he walked around the cart, right to the fire where we sat stirring our quail stew and fiddling with a cowbell, a eucalyptus limb carved with crows, and a rubber rain boot, respectively.

"I thought pilgrims did it for religion," Henrymoss managed through a dry mouth, after a moment's staring at the blue tattoos all over our hands, corresponding with our names; our beards like nests, our clothes which were simple robes like monks once wore, very rough-spun and sturdy, all mottled shades of brown and red.

Perches looked up at him solemnly, his big brown eyes sharp in that skinny, hawkish face.

"Oh yes, indeed. We have each chosen our worship, our path to perfection. You see." He held out the carved eucalyptus stick. The crows etched into it were glossy, impossibly detailed. "This," said Perches, "is where they are at ease, in a perfect balance with the wind, the light, the bark. They know exactly the branch. Is it not what all men and women seek?"

Boots stood then and slapped a broad hand on Henrymoss's back, laughing. The boy jumped.

"This fellow is full of shit." He winked. "It is my way that is holy. The Boot. How is it we tramp through the world? The Perfect Boot is the perfect union of foot, earth and path, weathering all mudslides, all asphalts, all heart-breaks. Come my boy, have a drink with us." Boots is the biggest of the three of us, blonde and freckled, with a flushed, round face and nimble leather-working fingers. Henrymoss noticed that he was barefoot, his soles and toes so callused and battered they looked like rocks. He sat down on a wooden folding stool next to the third of our number, Bells, who polished a coppery cow-bell in his lap, and poured Henrymoss a glass jar full of wine. Bells looked up at the boy, grinned, showing three missing teeth like black doorways, and rang the cowbell.

"Listen," he said. "The bells toll in and out the ends of the world. Did you know that? Have you heard that they carried Bells, all those players, and their Lyoobov?" He ladled soup into a ceramic bowl and offered it to Henrymoss.

"Hey kids!" Bells yelled, whistling two tones through his three missing teeth. "Come out from behind the cart, come sit and have a bite and a tale."

Henrymoss took a big gulp of his wine, hoping it would make him look at ease and adult when they came. It was sour and strong in his mouth. The girl Jay was the first to pop her head around the side of the cart, hair making a spiked blue silhouette with the late sun behind it. She darted, taking leaps through the meadow. Two boys, Jeremiah and Samfir, followed her, and then slowly another girl, the small one called Mouse, though her real name was Mara, who could climb a tree faster than anyone, who always stuck her hands in holes in the ground first, just to prove she was tough, and did not deserve to be called Mouse. Still, her hair never grew longer than a thick fur, her ears were rounder than normal, and she was short; it stuck.

No one else followed. They'd crept back to the trees, to tell their brothers and their aunts—something new has happened, something strange. Throw dimes and old wires into the fire, leave out the wishbones for the old women with bobcat tails who live in the brush. Come see, come see! One girl hung about at the edge of the wood for a moment after the others had fled, staring at our dark-eyed cows with a silent, bright kind of hunger which she at last, with some difficulty, swallowed down, running after the others under the arms of the bays.

And so it was only the four children called Henrymoss, Jay, Jeremiah, Samfir and Mouse who sat around our fire, we wheeling seekers of the True Path, all walking it together though our grails are many. A pipe full of strong tobacco was produced, and a set of fine china plates wrapped up in a child-sized quilt, tied with gut string. Perches fetched silver forks and knives from the inside of the cart, kept in a box lined with velvet full of slots and bands to keep the cutlery separate.

"Like corralling horses, ducks and pigs," said Boots, handing each child a fine white napkin, a porcelain saucer-plate painted with fading bucolic scenes from a long distant rural past—neat brick farmhouses, maids in gowns, gentlemen on horseback—and a set of silver, buffed to a bright shine. Amidst our ragged simplicity, this supperware felt bewitched, molten in its fineness to the children. Like holding the stolen wares of a king from a story they thought was made up, but had turned out to be real, there amidst a rough whispering meadow, beside a blackened pot of stew and a cart all hung with bells and leathers and scratched by the talons of raptors.

They were used to eating from flaking clay bowls fired in the kiln down near the ocean, which many villages shared. The bowls had to be thrown back to the ground after a few weeks because they started to crumble to dirt. In some hamlets, the women wove baskets, small ones the size of plates. These lasted. Everything tasted a little bit like grass or ground. Abalone shells found on the shore, or metal bowls, plastic jugs that could be sliced open, found in refuse piles or by ancient suburbs, were precious.

The children's hands felt weak as they held that china, stroked the glaze with their fingertips, stared at the silverware, all its curves and prongs.

"Where did you get these? Did you have to trade something very special, like a cup of your own blood?" It was Mouse who spoke, looking at her own reflection in the polished spoon, how the flames from the fire turned it orange. A small sigh of relief passed from Jay to Jeremiah, Samfir to Henrymoss, that someone had spoken. They'd been afraid of dropping the plates because of the sweat on their hands and the way Perches, sitting directly opposite, watched them with perfect stillness, just like a peregrine falcon does a hummingbird, hooked, sharp, waiting, his nose very pointed, his eyes so light a green they were almost yellow, his hair a sleek brown fringe.

Mouse avoided Perches' gaze, speaking instead to Boots. He seemed to her the sturdiest of the three of us, the most kindly, with big freckled hands and a broad felt hat which he had threaded with wild irises. She was probably right in thinking so.

"This cart, my girl, has travelled distances on its wheels you can't imagine. On the highways, freeways, all the broken up asphalt, the fireroads, dirt roads, desert wastes. Oh my poor child, how big it is. Oh my children, how sad it is. You wouldn't understand this kind of sadness, not yet. Some places, there's not a soul but the crows and rats and raccoons, and old houses full of wine glasses that have not broken even as maples have grown through the roofs. I don't know why some places stay whole, and others break into a million bits. You are blessed here, the soil is fertile, the nettles grow thick, the bobcats hunt for brush rabbits at dawn, the Fools rose up from their camps and because of it the egret-women and buckeye-men, they've come back."

Mouse kept polishing her fingers over the spoon, but was leaning forward. Boots' voice has a rasp to it; he's the one who smokes most of our tobacco. Henrymoss felt Jay's shoulder against his, electric there, like a blue light was under his skin, as blue as her hair. He felt dizzy as he listened. Her smell of berries and a girl's sweat tangled in his imagination with Boots' words.

"My little loves," continued Boots, "this is the Place Where All the Waters Run to, did you know that? Your Bay is like a big kidney, draining out all the land and what the waters bring across, from the high mountains where the snow is and the clouds drop their rains, through all the flat Valley. Oh the Valley, our wheels moan when they cross it on the old interstate now slick with dust and shattered glass—there is a great grief in that place, my little ones, because so much was covered up with that black stuff, that asphalt, so much water was dammed and is still dammed, or dried up. Oh my poor little ones, my heart, the Valley has had its soul taken out, with no more hope of Flood. I have heard, it is said, that long ago there were tules. It was a waterscape of egrets and beavers and the leaping legs of frogs, the cottonwoods, the wild grapes, the birds who came every winter. Can you imagine, your soul cut from your body and dried up in puddles, after such fullness? I have never seen so many ghosts, so many straight lines of old fields where they once grew food in squares like the squares of houses." Boots stopped suddenly, looked around at their solemn faces and their sweaty hands on the china plates. He laughed and began to ladle soup with meat into the saucers.

"But as to these dishes, well. It is said, my willowy chits, because I say it, that at a crossroads heading into an old desert town named for an older saint, we three pilgrims, then seeking a Boot of Kidskin and Cactus Thorn, a Bell that Rang the Neck of a Longhorn Cow, and the Perch of the Dusky Hawk, we came across an old woman."

The children took small slurps of the soup, richer than anything they'd ever tasted.

"You could tell she'd been a looker," interjected Bells, swallowing his wine and pushing the long braid of his hair over his shoulder. "She'd been fierce, with eyebrows, now wild with age, that bushed and flared, dark red skirts of leather that we thought she might have dyed with blood." He winked at Henrymoss, who blushed. Boots laughed again.

"Yes, Bells, we all know you had a thing for that old wench, you'd have taken her to bed with you if she'd been a few decades younger, eh?" Bells wiggled his middle finger at Boots and finished slurping his soup through the holes in his teeth. Then he picked up a pair of chimes and began to tickle them with his fingers as Boots kept on with his telling. The children sat, soup spoons still, listening. We always do have that effect.

"This woman may or may not have also been some cast-off dream, some goddess of another people and time, part red-fox, part patroness of kilns and glazes. All I can say, my small fellows, is that she lived at a crossroads in a truck rusted completely orange, so that it looked like an ember, and there she kept trunks of the most beautiful china you've ever seen. Twelve bighorn sheep pulled her truck, and four more pulled her trunks of china, on little perfect red wheels. Don't ask me why all that porcelain didn't break. She told us she always set up shop at intersections, stayed for a moon or two, then carried on. Her plates and silver she had collected from empty houses and collapsed restaurants as far as the roads and her sheep would take her. She was a bit like us, really, just gathering dishware instead of boots, bells and perches." Boots came and sat down right beside Henrymoss. The boy inhaled, and smelled his tang of sweat and also that something sweet and dry, which always hangs around Boots, like sage.

"This was years ago," Boots continued. "One uprising of Fools will loosen the screws everywhere, as far as the fault zones stretch, fractured like broken bones. One uprising is like sending alcohol through a fresh wound, it seeps down all the rifts and cracks, wakes things up. A searing awakening. So, it was after that, of course, and who knows what hole in what abandoned city she'd walked from. Anyhow, mainly we liked that china, because we liked the idea of entertaining guests. Hospitality, that's an ancient virtue, one hard to come by now. What are pilgrims without stories to tell, and how can tales be told if a feast is not hosted, and must not one's guests eat off the best plates? Well, we traded for those dishes, this box of silver. Traded things far worse than blood, my child."

Mouse gasped a little, despite herself.

"Like several dreams, for instance, cut whole cloth from the psyche. She took one from each of us, a snip of transparent blue scissors. And she took a pair of very special boots, made from the skin of a pronghorn antelope six hundred years old and long extinct by then, a bicycle bell, the limb where a northern spotted owl had perched in the Douglas fir forests of the river far to the North, where the Redwoods once grew. These are like organs to us, you understand—like giving away part of your heart. But what, after all, is the point, if not to trade one precious thing for another, and keep moving?

"So there you have it. We wanted to be gracious hosts, feeding tales and tidbits from smooth-painted porcelain. It seemed so genteel, so outlandish, so important."

Dusk had come by the time Boots fell silent. Stars pushed out here and there straight above them, like the eyes of gray foxes, yellow and clear. Only Mouse had finished her soup, having a big appetite and more courage than anyone supposed. The other children had barely lifted a spoon. The way Boots spoke, and Bells tinkered with his chimes, and Perches lifted his hands, just so, against the flames of the fire, shaping shadows on the side of the blue and gold cart, had them fixated. Ours is a subtle hypnosis. The brothers Samfir and Jeremiah held hands in the growing dark, not certain if the feeling roosting in their chests was panic or wonder.

"They're not poison," laughed Bells, putting down his chimes. "Won't turn you to stones or songbirds or sap, don't you fear! Finish up, it'll have gone cold. Eh, Boots? Hosts must tell tales after dinner, not before or during. You ruin the meal."

Mouse watched as the others dipped in and tasted it, so rich and spiced, so good they almost choked. Flavors no one had tasted in the villages for centuries—cinnamon, black pepper, cardamom. The buttery flesh of quail changed to something exotic.

Perches reached his arm straight into the air, suddenly, and a northern spotted owl landed there, hooting gently.

"She is the last known in the world," murmured Boots. "He seeks the Perch where her mate will land, to give her a perfect egg. He may never come;

she may never find him. It was her Perch he gave away to the woman with the orange truck for the china." The owl looked at each of them, one at a time, and her black eyes were peaceful and bright.

It was then that Henrymoss spotted his mother and father, his little sister and his aunt; that Jay saw her grandparents, Mouse her father and uncles, Samfir and Jeremiah their parents, and amidst them others from the village called Nettleburn because of the thick stands that grew up at its edges in late winter in spring. The women knew how to cook the nettles into tinctures, teas and liquors; how to cook them with eggs, with ground up seeds; every imaginable way, and pounded and spun to string too. No one got stiff joints in old age, from all the nettle stings. The people of Nettleburn were gathering at the edge of the field, stepping through the nettles, trailing out from the village like wisps of smoke.

Henrymoss saw Alice, the woman with three fingers on each hand who played flutes when there were dances in the meadow. She always walked with a cane and a gopher snake sleeping against her neck. Mouse saw the girl people called Little-Wheel, whispering about the Wheel of all the stories, because she was hunched, one hand twisted and curled so much it looked like a wheel, though it didn't really have spokes, and it didn't spin. Jay saw the man who baked cakes from peppernuts and acorns and traded them in pretty packages tied with red string for nettle liquor. He was walking holding the hand of Jocelyn Strong, once called Joe, who now wore long skin gowns and wild roses in his pony-tail. Jeremiah saw the woman Anise who'd come to Nettleburn as a teenager, run away from somewhere north where the forests were darker and knives still easy to come by. She was tall and long of limb, with breasts that stood up and moved against the edges of her shirt, black hair always in three braids thick as ropes. He was only eleven but he always found her with his eyes, and it made him feel hot down to his heels. His brother Samfir spotted the man who was a sole reader, Old Bishop they called him, because he burned the resin of bishop pines when you showed him your bare feet and he traced their roads of lines with his twelve fingers, told you what they said though he was blind, and got himself around in a wooden cart pulled by gray geese; his legs were shrunken, spindly as brambles. There were others between—someone's sister breast-feeding a baby and chewing a dandelion root, someone else's son flirting with the daughter of the man who baked the peppernut cakes, always in leather aprons and a bit round from eating lots of them.

Behind them all, Mouse saw the Wild Folk, who everyone was afraid of but also deferred to, like deer to lions. They'd heard too, that Something New Had Come. They looked mostly like villagers, but their shadows in the moon and firelight made Mouse shiver. They had the shadows of wild things —mushrooms, wolves, coyotes, stags, egrets, mountain lions, hazel trees. Their bodies were part creature too, part vegetable, but part person as well, crowned with the pieces of a shattered world: headdresses of electrical wiring or broken lightbulbs, crowns of gutter piping, waistcoats of shredded plastic bags cut and folded like lace.

"Look what you've brought," whispered Bells to Henrymoss, who turned red and looked pleased. He felt Jay's eyes on his face, so blue he knew if he looked at her he wouldn't be able to look away, so he didn't. Bells stood, smoothed his brown robes, raised a shining bell as black as the round black eyes of the owl seated on Perches' left shoulder, and rang it once.

The sound moved through the bones of everyone gathered around that blue and gold cart, that hot embered fire. It moved through everyone like water turned to wine. It was heady; it took them by the spine.

"Closer my pretty Fools, closer you nettle-stung ramblers, you nursing mothers and keening fathers look, your children are braver than you. They've eaten from our china, they've eaten from our silver knives, our forks and spoons. Gather round, we ask for nothing from you, only that you listen if you are brave. Hospitality is a high art and good for any foolish soul. We feed you tales; I will ring and tell, Boots will polish each one like a shoe, Perches, he will make for you the shadows, owl-winged, a puppetry of feather and of hand. We are humble pilgrims long on the road. Let us rest our wheels near your hamlet for a little while, let us ring you our Bells, walk for you the Boots of our tales, show you the highest winged places where the owl and the kestrel perch in your lonesome soul." Bells' voice rang through his missing teeth like a bell, deep and clanging and stirring up all the dust in all the attics of all the hearts.

The ragged crowd of thirty, maybe more, inched nearer. Blankets were laid, nettle liquor sent to the front to be handed to Boots.

"Henrymoss," said Bells, and the boy lurched, and Jay's hair touched his cheek.

"Yessir?" A gasp.

"A gift for your mother, for raising such a curious and reckless little lad, who'd be the first to sit at the fire of strangers." It was a tiny bell the size of a hazelnut and similarly shaped, a cream-gold color, with a wooden clapper. When Henrymoss rang it softly, the sound pierced with sweetness, sweeter than any lemon blossom growing in some abandoned lot, a piercing sweetness that was full of thirst. His mother looked up from where she sat in the front of the crowd on a felted blanket edged with yellow embroidered flowers. Jay took Henrymoss's hand in hers right then, fast, both their palms damp, and he was so full with the feeling of her hot fingers that he didn't notice how his mother looked straight past him and at Bells, how her hand loosened from his father's hand, how her eyes turned bright and flushed.

Bells winked at her, and we began our tale.

"It is said, my sweet-blossomed lot, that in the beginning, the universe rang like a bell as it perched in the dark, waiting for its boots."

Anja Born of the Buckeye

I KNOW, MY WIND-WORN FRIENDS, MY HAWK-EYED LADIES, THAT THE story of Anja Born of the Buckeye is a household standard, a lullaby for your wrinkly mewling babes, your restless six year olds, the ditty you sing while scrubbing your pants in the creek or gathering twigs for the fire. It's that sweet story we use to make us happy, when sad ghosts pick up and walk the cracked Highways before dawn; when women with the hunched backs of grizzlies come out of their tunnels and take, now and then, a line of laundry, a pet dog, a wayward daughter. You tell yourselves the sweet song of Anja because sometimes you wish for Before, when the Tool Sheds stood, when cracks in the sidewalks had not been pried open, when the souls of all wild things were still in forced hibernation. Because you know by now, my sorry lot of fools, that living in a world where rocks have wants and will trip you up with a cane of quartz, a cackle, if you ignore their desires, is exhausting work, and quite unsettling. It might be easier to just go to sleep, to shut it out, to stop listening. You find you can understand how things got to be so, before they Broke, and sometimes you long for those times, and so you tell yourselves the happy story of Anja, to make it easier, to make it worthwhile, to smooth over the bumps. Because it is sweet, and it is pleasing, like the new salmonberry blossoms, such a dark pink.

Well, my barefoot black-eyed does, my tatterdemalion crowd, you sinners and you saints, I have here in this cart the true story of Anja Born of the Buckeye, the version told me while Boots was out tramping and Perches out climbing to the tops of trees to feel that aerie air, to dream those aviary dreams. It was told me by an owl who may or may not have once been a woman, who may or may not once have been there when Anja herself was born.

This is not your lullaby, though it is close. I'm sorry to disappoint, but I will, and that's just that. Same rootstock. It takes place only just after the uprising that was stirred like a pot of root stew by Iris, Ffion and Wheel—only a matter of hours, really. Like waiting for a ready seed to pop its head above the soil line.

You know already, of course, about the gathering of Fools—handless, three-breasted, wheeled, blue-skinned men and women, people who had the touch of otherworldliness upon them, the doorways of wildness open in their guts. How the woodrats and brush rabbits, the coyotes and salamanders followed those marching Fools by the dozens through the tunnels, how the owls followed them through the air. How they set fire to the Sheds that were full of Tools, and with that fire a fierce and tree-shaking fervor danced and sang through all those who were full of smallness and hate and greed. It sent them straight to a madness from which they would never return. This is the Power of Fools, the line they walk, the pact they've made with lunacy and her mother, the great silver moving moon, solace of all things chained and silenced in the world. The greatest power of Fools is madness. It is a thing they can swallow and sing. It does not break them as they are already hitched open. It does, however, break a man made only of greed, a woman made only of power.

You know already about the young boy Martin and his Miracle Frances, the thumb bone of St. Francis of Assisi, singer of fish and fowl. You know the songs of his friend the Fool. He was handless, the keeper of seven rabbits that glowed like glowworms in the tunnels of the underground. How the moles below dirt turned bone again to flesh, and Frances, reborn, spoke to those moles who were in some way his mothers and his fathers, and at his request they dug networks of tunnels, each emerging at the base of a Tool Shed, until all one hundred and nine camps had been mapped, and the Fools could march. The roots of oak, buckeye, fir, alder, the lace-runners of mushrooms, wriggled in the tunnels as the Fools passed. They wriggled with relief. Those tunnels echoed as the sheds burned with lunatic music, songs of loonery so weird and so beautiful, humming the ground like a giant jaw harp, that madness got into people right through the soles of their feet.

You nod. You know these tales. You are impatient for Anja, the girl of all your lullabies, sweet beacon of buckeye and change. You've been told the tree itself birthed her, pollen and chlorophyll dusted, from the flesh of a nut—a spontaneous and virgin birth, bark and burl to babe, a sort of miracle, a sort of thank you present from the souls of all things wild and freed. A sign that our kind was again a part of the family of things. You've been told that after Anja, the women with egret necks or grizzly bear backs, the men of granite vein bones, of black-tipped tail, of coyote eye and very long smoking pipe—all the forgotten ones, the in-between wild things, returned. Took up residence in collapsed houses. Sold bone broth from the thickets of manzanita, ladled out of impossibly fine baskets. Redrew the lines of our world, remade our mythologies, my fine friends, put us in our place. Because the Fool's Uprising, and Anja's birth, had opened the cracks up again, the doorways through the hedge, the rusted trunks and shadows. Let magic come out like an earthquake racing along the rifts of the world. We live now in a place of crossroad crones and woodrat circuses, a world where you have to leave pennies polished with lemon juice at the mouths of badger holes, bee pollen at the bases of oak trees where blue jays are raising their sapphire chicks, vials of fermented huckleberry juice at the openings of sea caves. Ah, yes, you smile and look at each other, you whisper, yes, he tells it well, but what about Anja, the girl who told us we belonged?

The story goes like this.

It did not begin with Anja, the brown-skinned babe of unusual beauty and perfect proportions. In fact, she had neither, but we will get to that later. It began with the girl called Wheel, whose mother was a wagon-driving witch, whose father was a spider. It began with the Wheel of legends, not because she was one of the Three, with Iris and Ffion, who gathered the Fools, but because she, my staring sons, was Anja's true mother, and no buckeye.

You see, it had been happening all along, a little bit here and there, this Opening of the Cracks. Magic got trapped in a woman's womb, now and then, like a fine dust. Back then, it was called Deformity. Or it was called Madness. Wheel, you see, was a Fool for a camp in the Alders, and treated as such, as a freak with a hunched back and bones in her feet shaped like wheels. A great menstruation of spider silk. She had already started to let it back in—the wild heart of things, shape-shifting, many-legged, blue-milked, painted in mandalas of fungus and grape-vine. Just by weaving those wheel-tracks through the tree tops, just by singing to them at dusk—the red alders and buckeyes, the Douglas firs and bays. Truly, it must have been in her mother too. She did, after all, invite the love of a spider who became a man just to tumble and hold her in his eight arms all clad in orange velvet. She always knew that all things have faces. She had never forgotten them, like the rest had.

Well, this Wheel, approximately nine months before the uprising of Fools, she won the love of several trees. They became men just to reach out and hold her hand. She was so surprised by her first suitor that a fit of laughter seized her violently and it lasted well into the night. The poor fellow was humiliated into retreat. He was a hearty young Douglas fir with fine green eyelashes, broad and thick arms, a suit of scaled brown, hair evergreen and spiked in its thousand long matted braids. He left behind his gifts in a whorl of her web and fled: a glass bottle of pure, thick resin the color of the long-extinct fur of the golden beaver of which Boots has seen a single pelt; the perfect skeleton of a red tree vole, those little rodents who once lived exclusively in Douglas fir branches, eating and drinking only pine needles. Wheel giggled only further at the sight of these gifts. It was hard for her to imagine a man, any man, courting her, the hunched and wheeled Fool who produced spider silk in lieu of menstrual blood.

By the third suitor, the fragrant and smooth-limbed young man who was also a bay laurel, Wheel kept her laughter in, a grin only. The girl had not laughed much in her life, and so had some trouble controlling herself once she finally had cause for mirth. Wheel had accumulated quite a dowry by the time she found the man who was also a buckeye sitting in the area of her web-tent home that she called the breakfast room. There, she drank morning tea made of Douglas fir tips, she ate bay nut cakes and she watched the sun turn part of the sky molten as it rose. It was the only place with a real chair, hoisted up on a thread—an old rocking chair she had found in a pile of wood and cement that had once been a house. The chair didn't really rock, but it reclined, and that's how Wheel found the Buckeye, legs crossed, enjoying the rising ember of the sun. He drank something dark and hot, like coffee, though this beverage wafted her way with the smell of dirt.

"Am I to have no peace?" Wheel said when she found him there, in her quiet morning place, a place meant to be un-breachable. This time she did not feel like laughing at all—at the absurdity of being courted, of being desired by men that were really trees, of being brought gifts of resin, wreath, soap, bone, treated the way women with smooth cheeks, fine figures, straight teeth, soft laughter, are treated, not crippled Fools.

This time she was annoyed. She did not want the gifts and their clutter, the rhyming words of love. She wanted to sit in her chair, drink her tea, watch the sun, stay separate from the world that had only done her harm. She crossed her arms as she rolled toward him.

He was the one to laugh. A dark, rich sound, many-limbed and smooth. When he laughed, Wheel saw the lines around his eyes and his mouth, tracks made from mirth. She saw that he was cream-skinned, dark red-haired, lean and graceful. He was so quick, she thought from this angle as he laughed, that his arms or his legs were many, and branching.

"I'm sorry," he laughed, "but you aren't very good at being stern. It doesn't suit you at all."

"If you knew," said Wheel, "how many of your kind have come trailing mud and roots and old leaf trash across my floors these last weeks, asking for my hand in marriage, as if I were something to be given away, as if I were some rare princess, as if I would make any sort of wife at all, for a man who is really a tree. Well it's absurd. I'm sick of the intrusions. I'm beginning to think it's all some kind of sick joke. I do not desire more ridiculous proclamations of love. I'm not made for it." She rolled backward slightly, tearing up a bay leaf in her fingers.

"Ah," said the Buckeye, uncrossing his legs, sipping the hot brewed dirt in the burl of his cup. He looked like he might laugh again, but did not. Wheel noticed that his eyes were green and as textured as a leaf. He showed no signs of moving from her chair.

"This is not a game to me, this life I have made. I have made this out of necessity. This is the only place I can belong." Wheel moved closer, and found that the Buckeye smelled sweet and smoky at once, a smell she liked despite herself.

"We have only come," he said, "because you've beguiled us with your gentleness, because you speak to us at night, because you play old sad songs with stars in them through your teeth, because you build your webs gently between our branches and never harm a twig, because we can feel your hands, and they are stronger and more tender than any woman's—and we have felt many hands, I can assure you of that. Did you not realize you had called us?" Then he laughed again, and stood, and gestured for Wheel to take possession of her chair.

"And of course," he finished, as she reluctantly sat, eyeing him, "because your father was a spider. We can't ignore this." The Buckeye straightened his waistcoat, which was a rich red-brown, smooth like velvet, but made of no cloth ever seen in this world.

"What does he have to do with it?" asked Wheel, curling her wheels against the legs of the rocker.

"He himself was beguiled like we have been. Right out of his natural form and into a body your mother would appreciate in the way that women appreciate the bodies of men, and not spiders." He winked. His teeth were very straight and flat, like a buck's.

Wheel blushed, thinking of her mother's stories, the eight arms, looking again at the Buckeye who leaned now into the top boughs of a nearby fir.

"Well," she said finally. "Maybe I'll let you stay long enough for tea." The woodrats who were her oldest friends had scampered up to her broad shoulders by then, and sniffed the air near the Buckeye. He held out a smooth and long fingered hand to one. In it grew, before their eyes, a perfect sweet nut, which was taken into small woodrat hands and eaten promptly.

"Magnanimous of you," murmured the Buckeye, and sat down cross-legged at her wheeled feet.

The next bit, my thistle-thatched lads, my wrinkled grandpas, my fox-pawed ladies, gets just a bit steamy. I'm sure you'd anticipated as much. I'm sure you can imagine better than I can, blushing, tell you. I'm sure you've guessed already that they never did have a cup of tea, they didn't make it so far. No indeed, because that wise and wily Buckeye, impossibly soft in limb and eye—what woman could, in the end, resist?—and thick with a smell of sweet smoke, he put a long-fingered hand on the flesh and bone wheel of Wheel's right foot. He stroked the spokes as though they were the perfect handful of sunlight his leaves had always craved, as though he were a normal man, not a tree, and this was the most profoundly beautiful foot he'd ever set eyes on.

Ladies, you can imagine the sensation that then rushed through that lonely girl's chest—or maybe you can't, never having been quite so different, quite so alone. What followed is too sweet for my words. What followed filled the whole day and the whole star-web of night, it engulfed and held Wheel until she knew not if she was buckeye bark and leaf, and he knew not if he was wheeled, webbed, curved as a human woman, and as strong. What followed called the stars down to rest on those great swathes of web that tented through the treetops, silken as buckeyes, round as wheels.

I leave them, the lovers, for your imagination, entwined. The great cracking open of the heart, like a glossy nut.

Like all entwined lovers, the robins, the chickadees and the thrushes of dawn found them. The Buckeye left her with kisses on her wheels while she was still asleep. In the cup made by his body in the web, he left behind a big, perfect buckeye nut, polished to the gleam of a planet. It was hinged, and inside carved with minute detail—a whole network of buckeye roots, winding and branched as city streets, such a vast expanse of pathways carved in that that single nut, they looked finer than hairs.

Indeed and of course, solid as any nut, there was a baby growing in her, and she knew it right away, how the balance had changed in her wheels. She carried that baby through the treetops, singing, spying on the robins and owls to see how they raised their eggs, their chicks. She watched the raccoons who nested up high, and the squirrels. How they ate the afterbirth, when it was over.

When Iris and Ffion found her, four and a half months later, Wheel was just getting round, her belly smooth and brown-tinged as a buckeye. No one tells you this part: that of all three of those famed witches, one was with child, rolling about pregnant and moody as a wind. It has been said, by those who know this version of the tale, that it was only because of her pregnancy, the mammalian tempers, intuitions, dreams, that swept her like fires, that the Fools of all camps were drawn in and grew brave enough to follow. It was because of her aches, her cravings, and that carved buckeye she kept always in her pocket, growing dreamy when she touched it, that she found the boy Martin underground, his handless Fool friend, the seven knowing hares, the thumb bone of St. Francis and the scraps of his wooden Chinook. And you know, of course, that without them no tunnel could have been dug or followed, and then no songs, humming eerie and twanging through the ground, no fires, no delightful and devastating waves of madness.

But no one except Iris and Ffion knew that Wheel was pregnant. She kept it quiet. Didn't want to be judged—a woman alone and with child. And no one guessed, since she was already curved in impossible places; no one knew that the great wheel of her belly was in fact the child Anja.

When it was time, the water broken, the contractions coming, she found herself wheeling out alone into the woods, on the ground, no webs to follow and feel safe upon. It was like being pulled, but by nothing she could see. She found herself at the base of a wide buckeye, in the heart of a buckeye grove, their branches a nest of silver and green, the ground around them sweet and smoky in its scent with the decay of fallen leaves. She fell down on her knees, screaming her sudden pain, and the carved nut rolled from her pocket. It rolled right to the base of the tree, touched it, and the bark, they say, curled back just like a door.

Inside stood a woman all cream-gray from her toes to her hair, and speckled with freckles the shade of buckeyes. She wore a big red shawl around her waist, nothing else. Her hair was piled in a wiry cream-mass on her head, and she was very old. Wheel had never seen a woman so vibrant in all her life, let alone one so old.

Deep in the root rooms of that buckeye grove, where everything smelled sweet and smoked and damp, like the man who had loved her nine months past, Wheel gave birth. The child came out in a soft-skinned buckeye pod. The woman in red rubbed Wheel's stomach and feet throughout, ordered her when to breathe and to push, like any good midwife, though of course she was really a tree. She knew, more than any of us do, what it was to bear children, a thousand at a time.

The babe called Anja that people gathered at the base of the buckeye to see, saying that she'd been born right out of the tree, was of course really the child of Wheel, and carried up to the branches and open air by the woman in red. Word spread fast, first among the great horned and the barn owls, then among the voles and rabbits and blue-bellied lizards they hunted, then the badgers, the foxes, the skunks, the anise swallowtail butterflies.

This is the point at which, in the lullabies, we say the first doors creaked open. The little gnarled people who were also chaparral bushes, stones, roots of dandelions, the brown and long-nosed people who were forgotten dreams and deities and wights of marsh, mud and nettle patch—they heard the singing underground, smelled the smoke and flames of the Tool Sheds burning, and crept out finally to see this baby growing in a buckeye shell, wrapped in a very quotidian checkered wool blanket. They brought gifts for the little Anja—buckeyes which they called her brothers and sisters, the sweetest pieces of stone, petal, ceramic, that they'd been coveting for centuries. A few of the Fools were brave enough to join those wild ranks, that truly dirt-smelling lot, clothed in tunics and dresses the same rich colors as their homes—green dandelion stems, brown gopher holes, blue pockets of sky. Everyone cried, like you are crying now, madam, and you too, sir. Even, they say, the sun paused and looked, and the moon too, as she rose at the other end of the horizon. The ashes from all the burnt Tool Sheds were heaped in the shirt loads at the base of that tree, and Anja cooed slightly, enjoying the attention.

But you see now, those old lullabies are not quite right. Anja was not born of the buckeye. We are not mothered nor forgiven by trees.

It was not that our kind was forgiven all in one go, and thus emerged Anja, proof of the erasure of our sins. The load of those sins is quite big and bulky to carry, but we must. It does no good to blame those before you for the world you have inherited, and then do nothing for it. No, our sins were not erased by Anja, not then or now. Anja was borne by a human woman, Wheel. It is true that she was fathered by a Buckeye, but the only reason for such a fathering was the woman Wheel, how she in her solitude sang to the trees at dusk, stroked and told tales to the woodrats, left gifts out for the stars. You see, she earned the love of the Buckeye, she earned it so completely that he walked out of his own bark and roots to love her in hers. It is true, little Anja was born just as the doors at the edges of the bramble-thickets, fallen houses, stone walls, were opening, but she was mostly the product of a mother's hard work, her lonely strength, her utter strangeness, her body once called deformed, her eyes which saw the faces of the spiders and the trees and called them family.

This is a story with a moral, my mother hens, my father ferns, my purple flowered lasses. But I'm no moral teller, I'll let you find it resting in your teeth. I'll leave you with it like we left the lovers, buckeye-slick and twined, full up and rich.

As for the babe called Anja, all I can tell you for certain is of that unconventional christening—owl watched, badger blessed, stroked by old underground hands. After that, her mother took her wandering the treetops. They say a whole village of men and women who were once Fools lived up there with Wheel and her daughter. That they made a home in the center of a great pinwheeling web attached to the tops of a vast buckeye grove, that it was like the striped silk floor of a circus tent, whorled with spider-silk nests where people slept, ladders where they descended, towers where they climbed higher to drink honey wine, make jokes and play cards closer to the wheeling stars. They say Wheel was a sort of Queen, her daughter a princess, with her arms curving oddly like a buckeye's, cream-pale and freckled everywhere. That she had five legs, all wheeled, slender and graceful as roots, which she kept under a skirt of silver so smooth it looked like moving water.

This is only one story. Others say Wheel and her child Anja were never seen or heard of again. Not a peep. That Wheel died in childbirth alone. That Anja caught pneumonia and never reached her first birthday, despite the frantic nursing of gray foxes.

It has been many, many lifetimes, and I do not know.

This, my sorry sweet souls, is all I've got. Ask Boots. Ask Perches. Upturn our carts, you will find that this is the end of my tale.

IN THE JUNIPER TREE, I WATCHED AS THE THREE TATTERED TALE-tellers, all wisps of starry smoke, sank back into the silent bark. There was the sound of a bell, ringing, the stamp of a boot, the shriek of a kestrel. My head felt strange, full of too many people's loves, too many sorrows. We were alone again, just the Juniper woman and I, sitting with my coffeepot between my knees.

"So, what is it that really did happen to Anja?" I asked at last, into the silver quiet. "She didn't just die, did she?"

"Death is never so simple as all that," said the Juniper with a crinkled sad smile. "But there's one more thing, little child, before Anja. There's one more thing and it's you. Who is Poppy, whose mother dug him out of the earth? Do you know that tale?"

"Well, yes—I mean—not all of it. It was a long journey, she said, and something to do with a needle, and then I was there in the earth."

"Your mother is a moon," said the Juniper. "Your mother is her own dusty constellation, her own galaxy of stars. What mother is not, whose womb is a cosmos?"

Suddenly she was very near me, quick and spry, with a sharp flint knife, cutting a thin line along my forearm. Blood welled, but when she reached out her knobbed fingers, she pulled a long thread of red from my skin, a cord of my blood. It stopped beading against my skin then, but my arm smarted and my head felt strange, to see a part of myself separate and glinting like that.

I watched the Juniper tie three knots in that thread, then hitch it to three creases in the bark above her, where flecks of gold still glinted like stars.

"Blood is always a pathway back to the start," she said quietly. "The parts of you that have lived in the past are ghosts too. They live everywhere, and nowhere at all."

A form coiled and unfolded itself from the bark, a final star-hemmed ghost. It was my mother, Molly. Like the other starry ghosts, she didn't look at me as she spoke, didn't see me at all; her eyes stayed with the Juniper woman, who was as old as time. But I, little pup of a boy that I am, I felt I was seeing my mother fully for the first time, standing there inside her own story like she stood inside her skin. She was so beautiful, my mother, because she was her own; because when she spoke, the place the Juniper had cut my arm throbbed, and I knew that she was also mine.

Constellation IV

The Mother Star

2301 – 2315 CE

•

Molly & the Baby in the Ground

I CAN'T DESCRIBE TO YOU WHAT IT FEELS LIKE TO HOLD YOUR OWN death in a needle in your hands. I got used to it, though, a woman walking alone all those miles through the grassland, the marsh, the evergreen wood, following the pricks of that needle against my chest, where it hung from a string. It was comforting, in a way, to see it there, silver and glistening, no mystery, just sharp and in my care. But the cost of slipping and falling was high. My feet became steady and very slow. I stepped each foot like it were a precious load, reading the gravel, the roots, the dust, through my worn out boots, to keep my balance. At night, I took it off so I wouldn't roll onto it and placed it inside a folded brush-rabbit skin, inside a sweater, inside the basket I carried each day on my back with my knife, my corner of flint, extra socks and the necklace my Sam had made for me seven years before, when we first met. Each bead was different, polished scraps he had found on the beach and carved round like dozens of planets: blue worn glass, mussel shell, whorled driftwood, orange plastic. In the center, my favorite thing: a tiny glass cow with a hole already through it, worn to plain white by the ocean, like it had been waiting for me, he'd said, and kissed the place just behind my ear as he fastened it.

I always used to talk about cows. Black and white spotted ones, or the beautiful brown ones called Jerseys, with black eyes and long eyelashes. That endless sweet milk. I'd seen them once, as a girl: the four cows that pulled the red cart of Bells, Perches and Boots, when they came to Nettleburn and told the Tales. I don't remember much about the Tales themselves, because I was so distracted by those cows, and their swaying long udders. "No milk," Bells had whispered to me after a tale, a melodious hiss in my ear. "No Bulls, no babies, no milk. Except for her." He pointed to the Jersey, brown as a new fawn, eyes more beautiful and shapely than any woman's. "Endless. She chews the cud of our words, sweeter than grass," he murmured, and took me over, let me tug at a teat until cream spilled onto my hands. I lapped it up like a little cat, and Bells laughed. The small bronze bells all along his belt jangled. I was probably the only child who didn't listen, rapt, to their tellings, to their hands casting dark shadow-puppets all through the trees and the kestrel that perched above them, now and then screeching. I was watching that black-eyed cow, named Hazelnut, and how she, unlike the other cows, did not graze idly, but listened to every word, blinking infrequently.

I told Sam this story the night we first made love—the fir branches above stuck with stars, a dry summer wind sweet as the smell of that cow and her solemn face.

I fell, after that, into loving, into that space that opens between two people, a whole country with its own stars, its own mountains topped with fog, its own endless, cracked tar roads.

In that country I lost my longing for the mystery of cows, the older world they came from, their strange fermenting guts, their wise teats, and grew a new one. The longing for a little baby—the longing I came to walk the hard roads for, needle dangling from my neck.

Really, it all began with Niss, our Wild Folk at the edge of town. She was only the size of my two hands tall, and lived in a small wooden hut, hen shaped, that hung from the branch of a bigleaf maple. She demanded that we bring her, every full moon, seven baskets of a dozen eggs each: ninety-four in all. She demanded that only women bring them, or men that looked like men but were really women in their hearts. Even if they didn't have eggs coiled up in their wombs, they knew what it was to hold a million breakable treasures safe in their bellies. She got each egg very close to her spectacled face, as if reading the shell. They were big in her arms, like a cradle or a giant melon. We never knew what she did with each, nor how she fit them all into the corners of her little white house.

I was barren. I am barren. The eggs in my basket were pieces of my longing. I gathered them with great care, always from the nests of beautiful birds when they were laying in spring—snowy egrets, great-horned owls, hummingbirds. I followed Niss's orders carefully, only taking one egg per nest, and saying special words I didn't understand but that she told us let the mother birds know who the egg was for. That this made them honored, and not devastated, if the egg was to be taken in by Niss. We didn't know what this meant. I only wanted Niss to be pleased, to hum under her breath as she took the egg through her arched door, placed it somewhere unseen and ample. I imagined that place was always warm, like the fire was perpetually lit in a corner. I imagined the corners of her white hut extending and extending, impossibly, like the walls were made of flesh and not neat wooden boards. I imagined each egg hanging from a net from the ceiling, wrapped in rabbit furs, and when she walked through she rocked the dozens of them gently. I hoped she didn't eat them, though nothing was certain in that regard.

On mornings when the sun was muted by fog, she came to her suspended porch with her cane and her hair coiffed neatly, and told us a story. Sometimes the story was short, a minute long, and we couldn't make head or tail of what she meant. Once, she sat there in her wool boots with her cane and said: my husband and I took the thorn from the hoof of the goat. When the house finally rotted and fell in, my husband he died with it. Our men, you see, guard the home. I have no red and felted cap. I am not bound to your walls. But oh, yes, we have taken the thorn from the hoof of the goat. I know you all have thorns in your hooves, and that is why you come.

Or another morning, when doves with their gray coats swayed in the boughs, cooing, she said only: there is an old old story. In it, a man hides his death in the tip of a needle in an egg, in a duck in a hare in a stone chest dangling high up in a tree.

All villages have a Wild Folk at their edge. You have to bring libation, as we call it. It is a kind of unsteady truce, though I don't think we understand them at all, and they know our every move. You have to bring the sweetest of gifts, or things will not go well—grass roofs will fall in on sleeping children, all the wood won't light, no matter how dry, fathers will start to desire their daughters instead of their wives.

I don't know what it was like Before, when houses were lit by wires and switches, and the water ran from silver tubes, but I imagine it was similar—you go to the edge of the woods, you leave the most beautiful dove egg you've ever found to make sure everything keeps running smoothly, you go back home. You don't linger there, for it is dark, and anything might be lurking, and you've never been very clear on Their intentions.

My sister lived with a man named Jonah a few miles away, down by the ocean at the edge of a big marsh. In their village the egret-women stalked the edges at dawn and at dusk. I was told they were gorgeous and it was hard to keep the men from staring, though their heads and necks were a bird's—from the shoulders to the knees they were women, tawny and with beautiful small breasts that glistened as the sun on the water glistened, as the minnows in their yellow beaks glistened.

The egret-women weren't interested in baskets of eggs. Every winter solstice when the morning was dark and low they took one man as a lover—all of them, one at a time. My sister always dreaded the year when, through the rain, they would stalk between the huts on yellow strong thighs, white necks moving and wet, and knock their beaks at her door. They said the men came back hot as embers, smelling of salt and mud, but wiser, and tender to their wives in bed, like they had been shown the feather-down secret of her soul.

My sister knew that this was what the other women had said, but she didn't want to think of him going there, being held by other hands; what if he liked it better than anything he had ever known? I did not feel so sorry for her—she had three daughters, little and spry and toothless girls who smelled of wool and appleblossoms no matter how long it had been since their last bath.

If a woman refused to let her husband go, or if he himself clung to the doorframe and shook his head, the clams vanished right then deep into the mud. The small fish were nowhere to be seen; the roots of cattails and bulrushes shriveled underground into chalky inedible lumps. It rained for weeks and the waters came up to the waist as people walked between huts and everyone had to rebuild. This happened only once, but it left an impression.

If we forgot to bring our lady of the Chicken Hut up in the maple her dozens and dozens of eggs every month when the moon itself was a big hen egg amidst the tiny hummingbird-eggs of the stars, holes formed in everything we'd made or used daily in our houses. Holes in blankets, in sweaters, in the seats of pants, the heels of socks, the fingers of gloves, holes in baskets, in our roofs, even in our rusty pots and pans. Egg-shaped holes that let the cold in, the mud in, the water out.

*

Seven years it was we tried to have a child, my Sam and I. Every month I bled red as I gathered the twelve perfect eggs. From the trees the gray squirrels with their white chests chattered and saw me cry. You'd think, after seven years I wouldn't cry every month the blood came and no small egg was growing in me, no small planet of life. It was like a ritual. The rhythm of my motherhood was a grief for the barrenness of all things that could not grow. I knew that the grasses and the frogs, the moles, the kestrels, the rare purple wildflowers, had started to thicken again and multiply since the lifetimes of my grandparents and even their grandparents. Some said you could feel it, a fecund stirring since the Fool's Revolt long ago, when the Edge People and the Wild Folk began again to burst out of moldering apartment complexes overgrown with blackberries, from rusted trucks toppled sideways into creek-beds. But there were so many things that would never bear their children into the world again, ones we heard of in stories but never saw—bears, otters, whales, redwood trees, yellow spotted salamanders and tundra swans. And the wild creatures who were around us—they were afraid still, and did not come near. Perhaps they had learned from their long-ago ancestors what we were capable of. They had not forgiven us. I thought of that final mother, and those final young ones—cubs, pups, seedlings, chicks. The knowledge of being the stopping point of an entire line.

There came a day at the end of winter in that seventh year of childlessness when the wood where Niss lived was still bare but the hound's-tongue flowers, blue as dusk, and the white trilliums were up everywhere, the coyotes courting out on the estuary strands, and I could no longer bear my own emptiness. I wanted a little one in me, to raise and hold against my breast like a prayer, more than I wanted anything else—my husband, the sight of the ocean from the bare hill, my own life.

I brought my eggs to Niss at dawn, before the others could get there. It was still the time of year when eggs were hard to come by. The women of my town raised ducks and geese for this purpose, docile white ones and mischievous mottled ones. They had pens but we were careful not to cage them—Niss would sour every last store of acorn and seed, rub egg-shaped holes into every last sock and roof, if she were to feel that those geese and ducks were prisoners. The pens were only to keep the foxes away at night—otherwise we herded and followed them. They knew they had a safe bed and roost, water and food, in the little huts we made for them, so they always turned back at dusk, honking, a pattering of yellow feet. That is the sound of the evening coming; it has been since I was a girl.

I had taken the twelve warmest, bluest eggs that morning, each as big as my fist. The walk to the wood where Niss's house hangs was full of the small watching eyes of gray squirrels.

She sat on her front steps, which dropped off into air, darning a hole in a knitted bag that looked like a large stocking.

"Good morning, Molly," she said to me, and looked up over her bright spectacles. "You are alone." She continued to knit, and I watched her for a moment because I didn't know what to say. The needles, wood on smooth wood, clicked. The yarn, spun from rabbits, flicked in and out with her fingers like the whole effort—hands, knitting, needles—was one moving animal in her lap, like a secret hypnosis, meant to calm even the kinglets to her side.

"I wondered." Instead of finishing my thought I lifted my basket and began to hand her eggs. She took the first one, greenish and speckled, smiled at its warmth on her cheek.

"Did you, now?" she crooned, stroking the shell.

I lowered the basket again.

"Do you know about fertility?" My body went hot and then cold as I said it, like I'd loosened one thousand muscles and bones at the same time.

Niss laughed. She pushed the egg through her door, set down her knitting, and laughed harder. It was like an old man laughing, the way my grandfather used to, with a wheeze and a snort, and the skin on his round face shaking. He laughed like that after dinner when he and my father had shared some of the mead my mother kept brewing in the kitchen—blackberry, nettle, rosehip, huckleberry, dandelion root. Or when we went to the beach to gather in the winter, every week together, and he was barefoot in the sand and gleeful at every small strange thing I would bring to him in my soft and girlish hands—a tiny plastic lizard, color wearing off to reveal white beneath, a long spiraling cord like the lock of a mermaid, he kept laughing, with deadly strangling hair, a heavy plastic circle with buttons, one embossed with a trumpet, and the letters BMW in shiny colors. "Useless," my grandfather would snort, and then begin giggling, and then the strong guffaws of hilarity, which only got worse as he aged.

Niss laughed like that. I could see her teeth, pointed as a mole's.

"Why is it," she managed, eventually, "you think you've been bringing me eggs these many years? What do you think I do with them? Eat them?" She giggled in her deep snorting way. "Why do you think when you dig for roots, you find them, swollen and sweet? Why do you think, when you gather berries, they are plentiful and dark with their ripest juices?"

"Then why is there no baby in my belly, and we've been trying, my Sam and I, for seven years?"

Niss stopped her giggling, straightened her gray bun and the loose wisps of hair, smoothed her hands across her sturdy red dress. Her dark eyes grew darker, and I thought I saw sadness there.

"Sweetheart," she said, in the tone of my mother. "Your wombs are beyond my ken. There was a time long ago and on another continent when my grandmother might have been able to help you there, quicken the seed and all that, but don't you know that by now your own kind has blown it? Maybe the alders and the salmon, bless their sorry lost souls, and the geese have had enough of your babies, so many of them. Maybe you've had your turn. I'm here to tend the fertility of all the things you've damaged, not you yourself. Seems you people still haven't managed to tend it on your own." The small old woman pulled a blue-green shell fragment from within the hut, and showed it to me, etched with a single tall rectangle, full of windows, full of faces that turned before my eyes to poppy seedpods. I began to cry. Not like the tears when I was alone and the gray squirrels watched. No, these tears felt hot on my cheeks, like they were making cracked highways. They felt salty and uncontrollable, as if to fill the place in my middle where a little one would never grow. It is hard to describe, to a woman who has not felt it, the need for a small curled being to grow under your skin, fed by your blood. It is as sharp as the need for milk when you are small, only it pushes at each red boundary of your heart.

"Look," said Niss. "Give me those eggs." I wanted to squeeze her between my hands, then. I know such a thought is some kind of blasphemy, now, but I felt it. I lifted the basket.

"If I told you," she said softly, taking up each egg, placing her cheek and ear to it, "that there is a way, but it's very dangerous, very old, and very strange, would you take it?"

"Yes." I didn't hesitate.

"Indeed. I thought so." She lifted all twelve goose eggs into her small house before continuing, seated again on the stoop, knitting. "I have two eggs deep in the crannies and lofts of my home. One has in it your death, preserved in the tip of a needle. The other, a life that you could carry. You must pick an egg without knowing which it is. Then you must crack it. If it is the one full of new life you must swallow it whole. You'll grow like any other pregnant woman, and give birth to a child with ten fingers and ten toes, though his nature I cannot speak to, nor to the possibility of a tail. If you crack the egg and find in it a needle, you can either politely return it to me, and go back home, and forget all of this business, or you can follow it. That needle with your death in the tip is a compass needle and can be followed to a baby that must be dug up from the ground, a birth from the roots, perfect and growing as a seed. If you break the needle, you will die, right there. You will need to carry a shovel, which have been banned and lost for centuries. No digging stick will do. Only a shovel. And don't ask me how to follow such a needle. I've never been so stupid as to try."

I didn't ask what a baby dug up from the ground would be like—a bulging root, a dark and wrinkled demonic little thing? I didn't ask about the tail of the baby if I swallowed it, or who its father and mother really were. I only nodded and tried to look capable. I set my empty basket on the ground.

"I am ready," I said. I smoothed my red-brown hair flat. Niss looked at me, sharp, over her spectacles, and a wind passed us both, full of ocean and the opening of trillium flowers. Then she turned and went into the hen-roofed house. She seemed to stay inside for hours, rummaging through halls and closets and tunnels coiled into that hut like miles of old lace. I thought about babies dug up, roots dangling from their feet. I grew afraid, wondering if the sharp and deep highways made by tears should always be followed. Niss emerged again before I could run away, with two eggs, each as big as her head and balanced on her palms.

One pale green, one pale brown with a spray of tiny brown freckles. Simple, unassuming eggs, like a hen lays, not the delicate beauty of a hummingbird egg, the scrawled heft of a murre, gathered from sea cliffs.

"You can go home still, you know."

I reached for the pale green egg. It was too perfect, smooth and gentle to hold the needle of my death, I thought. Only a soup of child could be curled there, waiting. It was warm in my hand, as if freshly laid. Niss's expression didn't change. I couldn't read her. She only produced a small wooden teacup, bowl-sized in her hands, and held it out for me to crack the egg into.

The white and yolk slid out softly, like any fresh egg, yolk the shade of a sunrise, a goldfinch, a fine ember. I reached to drink it, shaking with a joy that whisked suddenly through me as strong as those winds off the ocean.

"Wait," said Niss. "Look closely."

I swirled the bowl in my hands. The yolk shifted, and there in the center of it glinted a silver needle, intricately wrought with an arrow at one end.

I couldn't tell you the names of the roads I took with that needle around my neck, nor the way my Sam looked at me when I told him, and left just as it was getting light, the barn owls still flying against the fading stars. He tied the string with the needle woven to it around my neck, kissed the knot against my skin, and wouldn't look at me again. I began my walking, first on the deer trails out of the village, through a stand of firs, then onto the cracked, hard road called the One, with the chips of yellow paint still flecking the center here and there.

I didn't know where to look for a shovel. I didn't know where they'd been buried, unmarked, years and years ago. My feet did the walking for me. I just went forward, and the needle scratched my chest when I turned down the wrong dirt road, the wrong rabbit-trail, the wrong old highway.

It was many months of walking to the prick of that needle drawing blood from the skin of my chest, making its own little runes. Moons full and skinny, yellow and white and red. I passed the cracked and collapsed houses from Before, town by town. I did not go in. I met a woman with the head of an egret by the salt marsh, and she offered me a herring made entirely of salt crystals, out of the great pocket of her yellow beak. I declined; you do not want to get bound. I met a tall and skinny man with a skinny and handsome face, a black cap, a slender black pipe which he smoked through his sharp teeth as he took my hand in his, asked if I would come back to the fields of oatgrass with him, show him my soft breasts.

"You want a baby, don't you honey? And a shovel too?" He hissed this in my ear, holding my hand against his palm, which felt furred. His arms were impossibly long. Everything about him was, his eyes too, long and golden. "I can certainly give you the latter, and maybe a baby too, if you'll only come, have a little kindness upon me. Many parts of me are long, you know," and he pressed nearer. I shoved him off although I was shaking.

"No thank you, sir," I said, remembering how you were always supposed to be polite to the Wild Folk, even men like this. "I'm managing fine on my own, no help from strangers." I kept walking, past him, off the cracked highway, up a hill where a trail full of gopher holes led. The needle pricked and pricked and I found myself in manzanita thickets, so dense I had to crawl. Behind me, I heard a laugh, a yipping howl, and remembered that the eyes of coyotes were long and gold, just like his.

At a wide stream I lost my boots to a woman, small and translucent as the water. She had mucky hair and flat teeth. It was a toll, she told me and so I unlaced, went barefoot through that water cold as grief.

Once, in the night when there was no moon, a thickness of stars overhead, an ache growing like a kicking body in my middle, I wished I'd gone and done what the man in the tophat had wanted. I dreamt all night of red shovels made of garnets from the heart of the ground. I dreamt of my mother and my own birth, blood coming out with the placenta like rubies.

I caught small birds to eat and saved their feathers and their little round skulls. I dug for roots and ate handfuls of the new succulent chickweed. My stomach became a hollow, and I dreamed of babies in it, many of them, not just human ones but dark-headed juncos, raccoons, fence-lizards, and somehow in my dreams my stomach and my womb became the same: whatever I ate I also grew in me like a seed when I dreamed.

I woke one day after a dream of owls gathering bones in my stomach. I walked shaky all morning, afraid, and toward noon I tripped and I fell while climbing up a fire-road. The dirt was all orange dust, hot and dry, with sticky monkey flowers and manzanitas growing big on either side. The path was full of sharp rocks. I cut my chin and my nose, big splits like claws had ripped me, because instead of breaking my fall I reached and cupped the needle. My knuckles tore open too. The needle pricked into my palm. I lay there for many minutes. I thought of Sam and the old cow bead on the necklace he'd given me, and the way, in the kitchen, he chopped everything so neatly even with a crude stone knife, in such small pieces, patiently, while mine were always haphazard chunks. I felt sick; I wanted to take back things I'd said—that it was him, something in him, that made no baby come. I wondered if I were dying. I could feel my heart racing against the ground and my breasts ached from the impact. I wondered if milk, wanting to come out, felt that way. I un-cupped my hands. The needle, silver and tiny, lay whole. I stood. The blood from my chin and nose and fists spattered the dust.

When I got my balance, and wiped at the blood on my face with the gray wool of my sweater, I realized that the hill below where I stood was a gentle grassy slope. I thought to myself that cows had grazed there once, a long time ago. I saw pieces of barbed wire fence on the ground in long rectangular edges. Below those hills, tangled in their old wires and scrubby bushes mixed with wildflower and collapsed drinking trough, streets emerged. Further out, the streets became dense and lined, one by one by one, with square wooden houses. You could see they'd once been cheerful colors—pure white, green, pink, beige, even blue, with brick chimneys and porches and a place for the car to go. I'd never been somewhere with houses one beside another beside another, lined up and shattered. It was like some kind of big cemetery. I felt like I could see all the old lives of people so long ago, kids hanging their heads out the windows and laughing, neat rows of hopes, childhoods, professions, roads. Everywhere under my bare feet was the tar, the whole place cemented over. I felt tight in my chest like the asphalt, thinking of all the things that had died and were smothered down there. I wondered if the people who had once lived here, on Magnolia Street, on Eldridge Avenue, were full of night-mares from the down-below ghosts; if sometimes when they looked out their windows they felt afraid of all the things they were living on top of.

I walked and walked through those straight streets. I used the roads and their sharp angles, not the side yards and back gardens, because I was afraid of who might live there now, what Wild Folk. What they would ask of me. The shapes of the houses were jagged and growing blackberries. I saw big lemon and orange trees with wild branches bowing over backwards with fruit in front yards. So much fruit, half of it had fallen rotten on the ground.

I saw a rosemary bush that had taken down the fence beneath it and was growing like a tree, its fragrant limbs reaching far out over the patchwork angle of sidewalk, thick under my feet with dandelions. It was blooming everywhere, such blue I had to stop. I reached out to rub my hands in it and smell them. We were always trading for rosemary, that old rare herb, used in everything—dinner, tincture, perfume, a satchel under your pillow.

I reached to pinch a single leaf, to touch one open blue blossom, and then I saw a woman walking down the path from the front of that house—a salmon pink one, with shingles like scales, the roof a gaping mouth of jagged teeth with a twenty foot angel-trumpet flower growing from the middle, windows with a sharp fringe of glass at their edges. A swallow flew out of one window as she came, then another, until six or seven deep blue barn swallows with their crescent wings were sitting on her head and shoulders.

Until I die, I'm sure I'll never see such a beautiful woman as her. I suppose it's not fair to compare, as she was not a woman like I am a woman, but an Other Woman who happened to look mostly like a woman. No hooves or tail or sharp front teeth, just a fine green fur on the backs of her hands and forearms. When I looked closely I realized this was really a thousand single rosemary leaves, pressing out her pores. Her hair was a big black coil, and it too seemed to grow the thick resinous green branches from its braids, blue and blooming, a mess on the top of her head. She was very round at her haunches, her breasts sat up high and perfect and moving under her dress, so you could see the tops, a golden color like her skin, and freckled. It seemed the kind of body to effortlessly birth babies, easy as lemons on the tree, one after another from those wide hips. She wore a dark blue dress, just a shade darker than the rosemary, and it clung to her as tenderly as if it were made of their blossoms, with green trim. I'd heard of saints, and paintings of them made in old lonely churches. She seemed like one of them to me, like she glowed.

"I'm sorry," I said, without thinking, watching everything female in me fall away on the rough sidewalk in front of her where the dandelions and burdock grew in riots. I wished to be a she-cat then, so I didn't have to feel compared.

"Little woman, looking for babies, always you come and pluck my rosemary." A raspy voice, rich of course, accented in a dusty way, like the accent had been held onto from a long time ago and was only worn on special occasions.

"We do? There are many of us?" I felt dizzy, like walking into a story; and I'd always been told you must never walk right into one, or your soul would stay there and walk it over, and over, and over, until you were mad or dead. I had enjoyed the idea that no one before had carried her death in a needle on her neck, looking for a baby; that I had some measure of courage. That I was somehow special and apart.

"Look," she said, and was suddenly right before me, leaning over the fence and around the huge rosemary bush. Its branches pushed into her breast. Her breath was a mix of lemon blossom and smoke. This close, it almost hurt. The barn swallows in their dark blue-feathered coats did not take their eyes from me. The woman's eyes were just the blue of rosemary. Her lips stained dark red. "I know, *mamí*, what your longing is. Jesus, I do. So many in the world have gone barren and died. Little mice who ate the salt grasses. The whales." She leaned closer, as close as lovers get. The black and rosemary coil of her hair moved on its own, like a snake. The green fringe of leaves pushing tiny from the pores on her arms and hands was bumpy and fragrant. "It feels like a big tooth in you, *mamí*, like it's gnawing and gnawing and sooner or later it will turn on your heart. Fuck, I know it," she said, and she started rolling a little cigarette. She lit a slim wooden match—I'd never seen one, so perfect—on the side of her bare foot, and began to smoke, gesturing me in through the gate. My hands were on my belly, thinking of that gnawing tooth. "Come in, you need something for those cuts," she was saying.

"Who are you?" I asked, at the threshold of the ragged, salmon pink house, remembering how I'd been told never to follow such a woman into such a house. Rosemary bushes grew in huge spires around the house and seemed to hold it up. I walked through the door behind her.

"Didn't you guess it already? I'm called Rosemary, or I was, when they were here to call me that. My people, they travelled here over this whole land and that sea way way to the east. Brothers who travelled all the way from Siena to this place, they milked the cows you know, so long ago. They brought me you see, in their hearts and their handkerchiefs, in the sprigs of rosemary their mamas put in the trunk beside the painting of the virgin, all blue and gold, in their dusty dreams at night. They planted rosemary to use in the kitchen here in this new land, they gave bundles of it to lovers or picked it and wished for lovers, wished for dark nipples under their fingers even as they made the cross when they passed their Virgin Idol with her rosemary blue cloak, her little babe." She was grinning, breathing smoke out her nose. "I'm all of that, yes? You see?"

It was beautiful, the way her words came out. I felt thirsty. I didn't understand her: the names of places, the Virgin with the child, but it all fell around me, tender and blue as her dress.

"I'm called Molly," I said shyly. "It is like teeth, gnawing, what you say. You know about babies, then?"

Rosemary took another drag on her cigarette, blew the smoke in a ring around my face, and winked. She dabbed the open cuts on my chin with the blue of her skirt, showing all of her thighs.

"You look sweet, little lady," she said when we got inside, sitting me down at a wooden table by a series of windows all smashed in and growing with small pink roses. The whole place was like that—tattered holes in walls and the floor, wrapped everywhere with plants or the muddy nests of barn swallows. Blackberry, broom, rose, crabgrass. One tall woodrat nest. Holes all over the ceiling so the light fell in everywhere. Pieces, the kind we collect on beach gather days, decorated all the bare walls—every color of glass and plastic in tiny pieces, glued, it seemed, in intricate patterns: a big whorled shell, a blue dove, a crown of thorns, a blue blossom, huge, labial. Barn swallows were everywhere in the air around us, making small high sounds. "You don't have much deceit in you. You smell clean." She squashed the ember of the cigarette butt between her fingers, then reached one out, fire-hot, and pressed it right between my eyes. I gasped with the sear of it. Then she ran her fingers over my bloodied chin, and the pain left. Later I realized that so too had the cuts themselves.

"There," she said, "you'll not forget me now," and her eyes were somber, welling, as if there were tears in them, though they looked dry. She produced a jug from a thicket of rose vine growing inside the window, and two plastic cups. Into them she poured something cloudy-clear and stronger than any liquor I'd ever swallowed, rich with lemon. Then she pulled a smaller jug from the thicket, this time full of some sort of cream.

"Cow cream," she said, and I stared, and the memory of that Jersey cow who pulled the cart of Bells, Perches and Boots flushed through me. "Yes, yes, she's mine, my own, Venus I call her." She pointed out the window as she poured with her free hand, cigarette now tucked behind her ear. There, a fawn-colored Jersey cow was grazing behind a fat sycamore tree. Her dark eyelashes moved gently as she chewed. I wanted to weep.

Rosemary mixed the cream in with the lemon liquor, then pulled a tiny pair of scissors up on a chain from between her breasts. She snipped two pieces of the rosemary from the back of each hand, wincing only slightly, a twitch to her eye. In they went, one to each cup, and before I could grow uneasy or move to get up, she'd grabbed my left hand, pricked a finger, held it out, a drop of blood per cup.

"Now listen," she said as if I wasn't already rapt and pale and quivering a little on the edge of my seat, wishing to be outside and walking in the resin of the chaparral, the only blue the sky above, not surrounded by it, cloying close and netted by its sensuality. Netted just as thoroughly as some young boy would be to the blue eyes of that most beautiful, most sad, woman on earth.

Black mass of rosemary hair, dark red lips, breasts like tawny moons, her smell of spice, lemon, smoke.

"Yes," I managed, knowing I was going to be made to drink that cup, and promise away something vital, maybe even the child I had dropped everything to find.

"I know right where this baby of yours is, in the ground, waiting for this little red trowel." She pulled a shovel out of a decrepit window box where more rosemary grew and dusted it off, also into our cups. "I can draw you up a map. I also know that little woman left something out which you will need to know, the old crone. Maybe she's forgotten, being dry of womb herself—that's why she wants all the eggs, hey?" Rosemary chuckled to herself.

"Why should I believe you?" I said, bold, because it was all I had left, that child under the dirt. Because I desperately wanted that shovel, and map, and all she had to give me, but I was afraid of what the cost would be, afraid of being tricked, afraid she was making it too easy.

Her face flushed like the ember of the cigarette butt before she put it out and burned my forehead.

"Who, little lady, do you think I am? What, *mamí*, do you think I am good for? Damn this sad old world, damn all the men who brought me here, and their wives, for dying, for forgetting. Jesus, how it changes. Look at me. I am the most beautiful woman you've ever seen. No need to nod, it's part of the package, part of the bargain, like your mama's small feet are yours. Hips, tits, hair, my rosemary breath—look, I am a woman on either end of mothering, suspended. My breasts are always full of milk. Once they left offerings for me, the women when they had babies in them. They prayed and said Mary and said Jesus, sprinkled rosemary, knew my face as the part of them that would be forever taut and wholly giving, in that act of gestation. What do you think I want you for—my dinner?"

"But why help *me*? What's in it for you?" I asked, nervous.

"You will bring my name back to your people. You will speak of me. You will tell them. You will tell them the way to me and my rosemary, so long as they bring a gift. A woman like me, I will die of being forgotten, of having nothing to suckle. Already almost have. I'll let the cow step on my head soon enough if you don't. It has been so long since a woman came all the way into my home and took what I could give. It's been so long that anyone asked. This sad old land has much need of mothers. Of my mothering. But it's nothing if it's not asked for." She paused, patted at her dark coiled hair. "And of course, there's this business of your child... I have some interest there, you see, but of course I can tell you nothing of it at all. Might be a false hope. But no harm in trying, no? There's just a token I need from you, to make sure you do it, you tell them, you repeat and repeat my name."

"What?"

She gestured for me to lift the needle off my neck. Terror pricked through me.

"No, my death, it's there."

"Yes, precisely."

"You could snap it, any instant."

"But why would I, unless you forget to say it, my name, to them? Why, and you a new mother nursing a babe?"

I gave it to her for that thought alone: the little one, at my breast, sleeping, sweet and warm, Sam stroking the crop of hair growing on that tiny head.

She pushed the plastic cup to me. A barn swallow darted to my shoulder. I picked up the cup. At my lips. I trembled, thinking that she had already known about this child, that he might really be mine. Then I said, "What's the second thing I need?"

"A broom. A little one, made all of rosemary—branch and brush. When you dig up a baby from the earth, it's the reverse of a grave, but you must still sweep it first, straightaway. And you must sweep the baby too, with that little broom, to get the earth off. If you don't, she won't know who her mother is—you or root or rock. And, hear me, *mamí*, you must sweep anything else you happen to dig, even if it's just a stone, hear? Anything."

We drank. It was a shot of fire and blossom to my gut. My neck felt light. The place where she'd burned me pulsed. Licking the last of the liquor from her lips, Rosemary leaned near and drew a map on the palm of my hand with the fine, sharp tip of my compass needle, held delicately. A dark ink came out of it with each scratch. I feared it would snap, and I would drop dead, but she only kept on scratching out that topography, humming.

The map has never washed from my hand, etched there with the needle of my death. The burn on my forehead has faded to a silver scar, the shape of a rosemary flower. I followed those directions on my palm back down the road, a little broom and a trowel in my basket. I began to feel light-hearted. It took me only a week to walk from Rosemary to the X on her map, in a little meadow with red alders and buckeyes flanking a stream at its edge.

The meadow was big. A baby under it could take weeks to find, I thought, and how do you know a trowel won't cut right through her like a root? I sat down. I felt cramps at my hips, like menstruation, only harsher. I felt warm there too, like that shot of liquor with Rosemary at her table in the salmon-pink shingled house. To the right of the X on my palm she had etched a tiny rock, a tiny bed of orange poppies. Dozens of poppies grew in the meadow through the grass. The rock on my hand looked very smooth, like the two knobs at the joint of a bone. I set down my basket. I began to search, pushing aside the tall grass and the orange flowers, scaring a vole, wondering at the scale of her map, if it was a pebble she'd drawn.

When I found the rock, two-knobbed, smooth, covered in pale green lichens, it was as big as my hips, sticking up from the earth like half of it was wedged under at a diagonal. The poppies grew around it fiercely, a fiery bright orange. I brushed at the area with my rosemary broom, like she'd said, though it was thick with vegetation. It was not a little neat gravetop, like I'd imagined, bed-shaped, obviously the location of my child. Before I stuck the trowel in, I felt sick. Nausea and fear.

I thought of Sam, and the baby covered in dirt, little rootlets at its feet. What if he couldn't love it? What if he felt betrayed? What if the tooth in me, sharp and gnawing, didn't go away? What if Rosemary snapped my needle, cleaning her white teeth with it, stroking her black coiled hair, before the baby was old enough to speak?

I stuck the trowel hard in the dirt. It broke a deep crescent, six inches down. I'd never used a shovel. The silver efficiency of it in the packed ground felt like some extension of my hand. My hips cramped again, like blood and an egg moving.

I dug for hours, until the bats started swooping and above them the soft stars. The trowel only removed small clods, and my hands were weak. After a few hours, I found that the rock beside the hole was a bone, big and deep, bigger than a cow's or a horse's by two times at least. I dug at its edges until I had pulled it free. I dusted it with the rosemary broom, got all the dirt off. Under the bone, the soil seemed softer, darker, like it had been turned. I dug up bone by bone with my hand trowel, thinking each one the white flesh of a baby. I dusted and swept them clean into the dark and the bats. The air around me smelled like rosemary from all that sweeping. I wondered if it was a joke: bones instead of a babe, death instead of life. I shook under the darkness, the sweat from digging cooling on my skin. My hole got wider and wider until it was almost four feet in diameter, and as deep.

By morning the skin under my nails bled. My eyes saw strange shapes in the dirt under my hands—first just the woman Rosemary, reaching out her cigarette-burnt finger to my forehead and to my chin. Then egret women; the man with the top hat, the long pipe, the coyote's tail, Niss drinking from egg shells like they were soup bowls, my own womb before my eyes, like looking at the womb of a cut-open doe, pink and red, taut, vulnerable as a fruit with the thinnest skin.

By morning, the pile of bones beside the hole was bigger than me. I imagined some pure white cow from the time Rosemary spoke of, with dairies, centuries ago. A celestial cow with endless sweet white milk, suckling everybody, telling us all we were forgiven. I found no hooves. I found a big wheel white as the bones, and imagined some old cart and plough. Delirious, I daydreamed of milk, digging, digging those small scoops. I hit the corners of a ribcage. I dug and dug around those long ribs, big enough for me to lay my whole bed within. Huge. Dirt was thick between them. I was careful, wondering at their size. I'd had no water in nearly a day. My head pulsed and swam.

In that swimming, I saw a bundle inside those ribs the shape of a creature's heart, a bulb, roots dangling from one end, wrapped in layers of skin like an onion husk. Under that skin I saw the silhouette of small shoulders, a small round head, clenched hands, curled toes. Nested in that ribcage like a rare lilac bulb. I screamed. All I can tell you is that I screamed and my body seemed to fill and then empty, fill and then empty, as I stared at that bundle, my fingers bleeding, my hair loose in its dark red tangles around my shoulders, my breasts aching all at once like they never had, leaking milk against the grey tatters of my dress, even through the grey tatters of my old sweater.

I have never given birth to a child the normal way, out my body, between my legs, blood, placenta, contractions, umbilical cord and amniotic fluid. I have only dug one up from the ground, my own son, and I can tell you it took every piece of my body's strength. When I pulled him up through a broken rib, sheathed like any seed, I ached everywhere a woman would ache, having just pushed a life out of her womb. And everywhere in the heart as well. The dirt all over us felt like our own blood, his and mine. And like any new mother, swept into the soft wrinkled skin of her child, touching the ten fingers and ten toes as I was, watching the little lungs fill like fluttering wings, helping to peel off that seed husk, I forgot everything else around me.

I dropped the trowel. I forgot the bones. I forgot the rosemary brush. I'd dusted every femur and rib with it, even the ribs that held my son, before I found him there. But in my arms, that baby filled me like the wingbeats of birds, and the sun through them. I could only reach my hands to slough off his husk, where all the dirt and roots clung, to peel him out, damp as a bulb, wrap him in the little rabbit-skin blanket I'd brought just for this moment, stroke his damp head, let him find the milk at my breast. It was hours, truly, before I remembered, before I looked at the rosemary broom and heard her say, "every root, *mamí*, every rock." By then, my little son was clean and dry as a whistle at my breast, I sleepy and fed by his drinking and a handful of cold water from the stream.

I did it anyway, in a panic. I brushed him. He cried because the rosemary was rough. It seemed silly, and I felt uneasy, remembering how it had to do with dirt, and roots, and maybe I'd been meant to sweep the little husk even before peeling it open, not his soft new flesh. The rosemary branches left thin red stripes on his skin. I wept when I saw them. I rubbed him with crushed wild plantain leaves from nearby and my own milk. I kissed the length of him, and he only cooed gently, unperturbed, smelling of rosemary.

Before even my husband, I carried him to Niss like I once had those baskets of eggs. I came to her opened in every way, like a doe who has been eaten and transformed, even her bones—into needles, each one carved. No shoes, hair full of flowers and dirt, grown red to my waist, grey dress and grey sweater in rags, basket battered and with a new load—Poppy, named for the flowers growing where he was born. She was there on the porch, placid, knitting. She looked once at the baby drinking from my breast. She never spoke that time, though I think she knew, as she cracked a small duck egg over his head with a sad look in her eyes. He kept drinking and didn't move a fist to wipe at the yolk.

To this day his skin is faintly criss-crossed with delicate pink stripes from the rosemary brush. He is fourteen now. He can't speak. Not to us. His mouth can't make human sounds, his tongue can't shape them. I love him no less than the moment I drew him from the ground and the milk leaked through my dress. He listens; he understands us, but he cannot replicate our speaking, our writing. His mind darts off. I see it in his eyes the color of dark soil and pale bone. They dart to the grasses moving in the wind, the nests of voles in those grasses, the spots where edible bulbs are forming before they ever show their faces above the soil. I see him speaking to the hermit thrushes and deep in the grass to the mariposa lily bulbs. I've crept up to listen only once. The sound scared me all the way through, because it was not human in the slightest. It was bird. It was a bulb-growing lullaby, creaking and minuscule. When he comes in I kiss his cheeks and he smiles at me like any boy. Sam sits by the creek with him for hours, with fishnets. They wait together, quiet, holding hands, amiable like a man and a tame creature, a fox that likes to sleep in your lap.

Though he speaks only to the hazelnuts and the great horned owls, and in voices I will not listen to, I have found what it is I longed for, the yolk to fill my old green shell. I am at ease now. I do not weep or stare at the silhouettes of trees from the bedroom anymore. I do not weep at my blood every month. I have found that this single thing—to care for, to raise—is enough. My breasts have sagged from his fierce drinking. My hands are worn from stitching new diapers, worrying when he is off long in the marshes, smoothing at his red hair. At night, I think of his heart, not mine, and sleep with soft and gentle dreams.

Every spring, I walk the women of my village to Rosemary. I walk them all the way to her salmon-colored home thronged with brambles. I suppose it is a pilgrimage of sorts. We bring her all the blue seaglass we can find from the beach. None of us want our husbands to come. We fear they will never leave again. Maybe one day we will not be jealous. She lets us each drink a whole cup of milk. She lets me run my hands along the neck of her cow. Sometimes when we first come upon her, she is so beautiful, she is so big, I wonder if she is a piece of the sky, calling down the clouds into cups, letting us look in and see that all things need succor, thick as cream.

The one stray piece of this story, the piece that sometimes comes into my placid dreams, is the bones that covered and held my boy in the ground. I told Sam about them, their size, the night I returned, and we lay in bed naked together, all of us, in the summer heat. Poppy slept. I murmured about celestial cows, exhausted, and he kissed my forehead, and smoothed his hands over my breasts, and slept too. But the next day he told his father, who had come visiting with a brace of rabbits and a green glass bottle from the beach. He glared at my child with unease, lit a pipe in my kitchen and said, "You silly woman, don't you know whose bones those were? And you left them? Addled."

I stared back at him, offended, cradling Poppy at my shoulder. I shook my head that I didn't understand.

"Lyoobov," he whispered, like we might be overheard. Tears caught on the wrinkles around his eyes. "Lyoobov," like a prayer. "From the Fall, the great dreaming beast. Didn't you listen when you were a girl, when Bells, Perches and Boots came through?"

I smiled to myself. I hadn't, watching instead the cow, whose milk, Bells had seemed to intimate, was full of all their tales.

Sam's father made me lead all of us back to the spot. Poppy stayed the whole time in a wool pouch at my breast. It took us a week to walk there, a straight shot now that I knew the way. And that map, besides, would never leave my hand.

I found the hole where I had loosely recovered the bones. The poppies were still bright, though a few had lost petals. Nothing was there. The hole was hollow and empty. Not a single vertebra.

Juniper

AND NOW, LITTLE CHILD, LITTLE POPPY WITH TWO MOTHERS, ONE human, one earth, now you have the beginning and the middle in your coffeepot. I, old Juniper, I will give you Anja at last, and you will decide for yourself if she is the end, or another beginning all over again.

It is said, because she said it, that girl Anja who shed her hair at the end of every summer like her buckeye father, she said it right into my old and folded bark—she said that when she arrived she was pregnant with a baby, and its father was there beside her, partly carrying her, so cold and tired were they. His name was Martin. She murmured that name fondly here, round and round the rings of my body. I know many long things, see, because of all my windfall arms, dry and hot in the fires the People make, but also because that Anja, dear girl, she crawled in here and she whispered her secrets to me like to a grandma, like to the mama she missed. She tucked them into my berries and my berries into my folds, into the roundness of my rings and their own tellings, round like the round and round Road the People follow and have followed, year by year, round the peak where the Last Glacier is perched. Their Road, they follow it like I follow around and around the rings of time that seem to begin as well as end in my very bark, my very dust-blue berries.

I know many things because of my branches, burning, because of her whispered memories, and because of the ones who have my berries in their bellies and watch the passing of the world. For example, I know what the black-tailed hare children saw the night Anja and her Martin arrived, because they had eaten of my berries. These, their thoughts, are a memory floating in me like a scrap of smoke:

In the snow on the mountaintop there is a woman pregnant, round belly about to pop. She smells like she has come all the way across the cracked land, the Valley once filled and drained yearly by two rivers bound up in tar. She smells, to we leverets who watch through the snow-covered sugar pines, like her feet have dragged through all the broken roads where once there was sickness and blood. It is not a good smell; we the leverets know the smell of danger, but it is only around her feet, where she has walked, and around his feet, her mate who is freckled like the nighttime gets freckled when there is no moon. He is the one who has put the baby in her. This we can smell very sweetly because we know much of such things. This knowing goes in with hare-mother milk, rich and heady, imparting no smell, so we may lay hidden for hours in the grasses, growing fast, drenched in the fertile sap of our mothers and the truth of Loving. This we smell about that little woman too, she who is tucked into a round hut, the kind the People use in winter.

We like those bone houses. The People sing about the Moon and her very heady milk to the bodies of our brothers and sisters after they've been caught and snared with blood-red strings, spit and smattered with salt over the fire, strong back legs eaten while between their teeth the People whistle little wild-mint songs for the wild hare souls to take back to their mothers, their cousins, their mates, their yet to be born babies, saying: "we know your Names, we will tell you of the Moon when it is time for us to eat your body, and your bones will be made into small houses inside which we will dream and those dreams will soothe you like your mama-doe milk did when you lay in the grass of your birth."

The little woman is in a hut of many hare-bones, and her mate is gathering sticks with everyone else. They have given him felts all red and brown, and skins, and furs of brush rabbit in his boots. And so he goes through the snow, padded and quiet as they are but at his ankles he still smells to we leverets who watch in the shadows like a longed-for place across that sad Valley, a longed-for ocean, which we do not know about except in the Moon as it pulls and pushes at our mothers, our sisters, our wives, and those tides of new ones, pink and soft-eared, flooding the grassy alpine meadows each May.

All the sticks the People and the freckled man carry on their backs are heaped onto a fire to keep the little mother warm in the snow, in the hut of hare-doe bones where she, sleeping, dreams. Those dreams touch the bones of hares gutted, skinned and consumed. We watching leverets catch scraps of her dreams, of a Mother with Wheels for feet, a great web like a Tent above the trees, a long, long Valley of broken cement and the smell of sad houses, and a barren dusty place where strawberries once grew where the little baby was made. In her mate, we leverets see long tunnels underground, and a lost father in him, and a love for the little mother who he saw born in the buckeye when he was nine.

It is the longest night of the year. Upon it we leverets watch this small woman call out once the word 'Wheel' as her waters break and the People gathering sticks stop and come near. From behind us, a hand comes grabbing, the hand of a middle-aged woman in blue felts and fingers dyed black from oak galls, dark eyes and the lilt of the Valley of her great-grandmothers.

'Come here, mamí, *' she hisses as she picks up our sister by the neck, sweetly, like she is a gift. 'Venga, venga, it is her time, and you must help her. You've got her story in your womb, you know this?'*

The rest of us run away as the new little mother is rubbed with the soft ears of the yearling doe and fed her blood. The birth begins. Behind us, we leave wide leaping prints in the snow, and a trail of droppings which have blue-dusted bits of juniper berries in them.

A berry and a seed passing through a body know all the things that body in that time, in those hours, knows. The body of a chewing creature—this I need, my alchemists, my magicians: the guts and the colons of the Ones Who Have Teeth.

*

And the smoke of burned windfall, my arms: this also knows that which it touches. So I can tell you in wisps a memory that comes now, little boy-child clutching your arms around your chest, little child who knows what it is I say. I will tell you a memory too of my smoke so sweet and hot that first night, when Anja gave birth and Martin was made to sit among strangers while his love screamed, because no men were allowed near. So he sat by the fire of my branches, ready to burst. I liked him because his hands gathering wood grasped each piece tenderly knowing it was alive, or had been, acknowledging some preciousness. This is the sign of a good man to an old Juniper who has seen so many, many centuries. An old Juniper who has drunk up the bits of poison fallen from the thick clouds. Hands that, despite the world, examined each new fallen piece happily, like it was a small present. His hands had love for that woman Anja all over them. The smoke from the fire of my branches touched his hair and his cheeks rough with beard, his layers of scrappy pant and coat—denim rags, nettle spun, rough wool. My smoke got underneath to his skin and his chest, down his nose and into his lungs and there, there was the thing they had carried up to the sharp mountains where the Snow Melts and Makes Rivers.

My smoke touched something in his chest that had been carried, like a tinderbundle wrapped with the dark green seaweed of their coast: they had wanted to bring the Word. Missionaries—that's what they carried up through the snow, shaking with hypothermia. Missionaries—a concept as old as candlesticks. The salmon told me about it long long ago—spawning as they once did upstream, all the way up here, with adobe missions, Fathers, Priests, Confessions, smudged into their bones. It was a concept wept into the streams by the neophytes who before were Miwok, Paiute, Wintun, Pomo, Ohlone. Yes, this concept I had heard of, one kind of people saying to another people—your roots are all wrong, your branches don't grow right. Here, our roots, they are Right, our branches, they are True. That's the only way I can explain it, see? Martin, beside the fire, he had that desire in his chest, and Anja did too—a thing they had built their love around, he following her as she Went on her Journey, she called it, to tell other people the Way.

Beside this thing that they had carried, there was also, near Martin's heart, the memory of a small man and a Chinook made of glossy wood and dirt, and this made me generous again to him, for that little man knew all about what my roots know all about, and that wooden salmon knew of water, and the line between up here and down there, written into her bones like it is into the bones of all fish.

All my smoke in his lungs made Martin cough, and the People handed him clear snowmelt water to soothe it. In his coughing I saw torch-fires lit and carried underground. I saw the steep hills and alder valleys and beach cliffs and lupine-touched meadows of that place of ragged wilderness near the big Bay. I saw those places filled with the smoke of madness, the smoke of burning Tool Sheds, burning Camps, burning balls and bells the Fools who carried the nightmares of the world had been made to dance with.

My smoke in him opened that other smoke, its own nightmare: how they waited underground, eating worms brought to them by the broad-footed moles, eating the roots of dandelions and stray carrot patches, braiding each other's hair into elaborate towers out of pure panic, needing to keep from losing their own minds, too. The little man made of the thumb bone of St. Francis of Assisi told stories from places that seemed to those Fools (who had been called and coaxed underground to Burn the Camps by the Wheeling Roundness of Wheel, by the beauty of Ffion, by the mad avian-architecture of Iris) like other planets in time and space: dusty missions made of clay and wattle and surrounded by the white lowing of long-horned cattle, stone hermitages in dry places with blue hot seas nearby and wild spiced herbs in the hills thick with silvery olive trees where men made careful calligraphy in books in a language as old as my very body—2,000 years—and meanwhile fermented cheeses. The one sweetness of that time underground, in Martin's memory, was those stories—he was the only little boy amidst all the Fools who time had battered.

My smoke moved past that underground in him and onward, in the oxygen in his breath, moving all through his limbs to flush his blood, and there, as in the visions of the leverets who knew the dreams of Anja, I saw the web-tent of Wheel. It was perfect tranquility, a ship drifting above the world, away from the cinders, the char. On it leapt a littler Anja, always climbing down and coming up again with checkerbloom flowers, with wild irises, paint-brush, creamcups, farewell to spring, tucked into the close-shedding stubble of her dark green hair.

There—my smoke touched it, the deepest thing in Martin's chest. A soft memory in his heart where brotherly love was always a small blue seed buried and ready to grow into a man's love for a woman, since the moment that reeling girl was born and held up to the world in the branches of the Buckeye.

Anja always sat beside him by the fires they lit up in Wheel's Webs, in that treetop Court of Fools where everybody had gathered who was afraid to go down quite yet, for fear that it had not worked, for fear that one Master and a Tool Shed existed still, and would contrive to chain each last one of them. Hand them a new set of polished stones to juggle and juggle, as if their strangeness, their "deformity," would keep the rest of the devils of the world at bay.

There, my smoke touched it—a particular fire when Martin was twenty-four and Anja fifteen. Martin was about to leave the paradise of the web-Court, towered, tented, strung with the blue twisting feathers of jays, wood-peckers, lemon-yellow warblers, for the Ground, to seek his father.

With my smoke in his chest and the swallow of snowmelt in an aspen-wood cup from strangers, his Anja screaming the birth of a child, Martin remembered that night when he first learned that he loved her, and would always.

By that treetop fire of his memory, she was warming her hands, long skinny fingers, a little crooked, and eating a dove egg with a small wooden spoon. Between bites she tried to mimic the cooing of doves. Lips pursed in an O. She did it perfectly, and grinned at him.

"Wonder what I said," she laughed, and swallowed more egg. "Hope not some kind of dove come-on. Watch them all come landing on my shoulders, turning to handsome pale little men. Would you fight them off for me, Martin?" Her tone curled and unfurled, a tapping of glee in it, and also that higher note of a womanly sort of wile. Martin realized she was flirting with him. Not teasing like a little girl, but flirting, expertly. Where had she learned it? Her eyelashes seemed very long, and sly, pale as moonlight. Martin found himself blushing, and Anja reached her hand to touch that redness.

"Ooh, jealous, Martin?" she laughed again, tossed her eggshell far, for the raccoons. "A princess may have many suitors you know. As my body guard you'll have to fight them off. Unless of course I like one of them." She ran her hands through her hair—luxurious and long, since it was spring. Robust, almost black, with that hint of green.

"Always," Martin managed, going along with the joke, pretending to make a flourish and a bow. He felt choked, all of a sudden flushed with sadness—that he hadn't told her of his leaving—but how could he? He would never be able to leave if she begged him not too. He was sad that by the supple fire, full of sweet fir boughs, Anja looked like she had walked right out of an old skin, and he hadn't noticed until he was about to leave. Even her lips seemed darker, fuller, as well as her breasts when she moved to stoke the embers and they swelled slightly, small but high, at the neck of her ragged yellow dresses, tucked over boxy brown pants. Underneath all those random layers he hadn't realized until now that she had shifted, become a new creature, as different in his eyes as a tadpole to a red-legged frog. Suddenly her fullness filled up the whole night, and he wanted to cup her face in his two hands, smell the roots of her hair dark as buckeye humus, put his lips upon her.

She caught his looking as she sat down again, reaching into her pocket for her polished gambling nuts—once, beyond the Web but still in the fir tops, several sisters, squirrel-women with long, thick tails and large teeth, had kidnapped her for a day, but she had learned their gambling tricks in an afternoon and out-betted them—five smooth hazelnuts, rippled, bronze, in her palm. A dart of knowing went through her, at his eyes. She put the nuts away and went silent, startled.

The next morning, Martin, who had stayed awake all night thinking of Anja, telling himself it was indecent to love her, being almost her older brother, climbed down from the firs and did not return for two years. When he did return at last, no father to be found, Anja herself had left.

"A Mission, she has a Mission. Got it in her head after you left. Her Mission," said Wheel. "Lonely child," she added, "some heartbreak"—a knowing look. Martin, he could do nothing but follow.

I have grown my bark slowly around the whispers she left, around the blue of my berries she tucked into these xylum folds, each seed with a bit of her story in it, proud like I was once when I was younger, suppler, no fire yet at my trunk, no storm to split me.

Take seven of these berries she tucked here, put them in your small silver pot. It is lined with the stories of the past now, and ready to carry Anja. Light a fire under it—yes, in here, in me. I am not afraid any longer of flame. They must be a right soup before they will release any telling to you. No more than seven—none of us is allowed the whole story, child, and I certainly can't tell it all. Only scraps of her, and of Martin, remain easy for me to find. There are thousands of others having their lives around me—bighorn sheep, black bears, rattlesnakes, night stars, columbine flowers, white pines, goshawks, hares, and all of that is in me too. I am not so partial.

Poppy

I GATHERED BRUSH OUTSIDE IN THE NIGHT. THE HOOTING OF spotted owls filled up the thin air, dry in my throat. My head was full, a night sky moving. I used the windfall of the Juniper. I made my fire inside small. I swept any stray popping ember back in. The smoke seemed to well straight up, further than I could see of her trunk, out the old holes made by woodpeckers.

From under the dust blue of her thick dress she pulled out two small cups, burls, and gestured for me to pour. What came out of that coffeepot was thick and steaming, with smells of resin and dirt and something delicious, like roasted nuts. It was blue. Sky blue.

"I have a soft spot for her I suppose, just a very small one," said the old Juniper. Her voice crept and curled around me, ringing and ringing the roads of her weatherlines. "Her father was a tree after all."

She lifted the cup to my cup—cheers, she murmured. We drank, and we became Anja's Seven Memories, stored there like diaries in the 2,000-year old xylum. I suppose, more accurately, she, across the fire, became Anja's Seven Memories, all weathered in her own smoke, and I listened so eagerly they may as well have been in me. She spoke them with her eyes closed and her teeth gleaming, and when she spoke it was another voice entirely, a woman's, human. I sat, hot, stomach turning and turning with that blue drink. I saw her, Anja. I swear it. I saw her at the same time as the old Juniper crooned out her berry-sung voice. I saw her around or over that woman like a sheath made of cobwebs, a glimpse of her with each memory. A young Anja first, not much older than me, all skinny and glowing, hair a velvet dandelion-spun halo, wearing the red felts these mountain people wear, weeping, ashamed; a much older Anja, silvered, grown wide like a tree grows, ears hung with a dozen small bones gilded gold. Glimpses, only, but I tell you I loved her all through. I understood Martin. I understood Bells, Perches, and Boots. I understood all of you, for your crooning adoration. And your eyes have not even touched her.

I think it made me become a human person finally and all the way through. Hearing her, seeing her, grew that organ in me which makes a person a person—the Organ of Sorrow. And not for the reason you think—not because Anja was an Angel, a goddess come to the mountain peak to bear her holy child and convert the ones who lived there. Not because I was seized with some religious fervor, but because I came to feel pity for another, to feel her griefs, to feel her heart all upturned in a thousand places, letting strange light in. She taught me where my heart was—not only that it moved my blood but that it had a human mother in it. Not only Lyoobov, no, not just the gray foxes letting me sleep in their dens, but more than any of these the one who pulled me out of the ground and nursed me all my life. I saw that maybe the rest of me had been made by accident by that owl woman once called Margaret, the beast bones of Lyoobov, poppy roots, mole snouts, the magma of earth and old fox dreams, but my heart—this my mother grew in me when she pulled me up like an iris root. This, her unsheathing of me grew, right there, stronger and stronger on her milk and her kisses and her stories full of flying cars and oceans with whales still in them, cows with milk like rosemary who could prophesy the future.

This—the desire to know the future—this is a purely human desire. I can assure you, no creature ever cares to know. But we do—that's part of what a heart is for. We look out at the stars and first feel awe, but always, after, panic, and then guilt—that we have been given Paradise, that we might fail. Again and again—what if failing is what makes us who we are? Age after age, killing off each other, or every other kind, no middle road, no path we know how to find in time. That this is the guilt you carry, and Anja at once reveals it to you and eases it; rubbing some salve on the weary shoulders of your soul. Making you weep for your mother, and the time you were small, eating wild blackberries in August with her to help you get out the thorns. Weeping for the day you could no longer let her, and had to do it yourself, and shoulder her, and your whole kind, and the world itself.

I cried. Yes, I admit it freely, I cried the whole time of Anja's Seven Memories. I cried because I am two halves. One belongs to Lyoobov and to the foxes, but the other is yours. It is Molly's. It is Sam's. It Margaret's. It is Rose's. It is Ash's. I, a human self who was longed for—Poppy. What a new concept that was for me! It is easier to be one day a fox, the next a newt, to reside in their calm. To be a son—this made me cry and cry. And to know that each fox too is a son—this made me cry and cry even more. My tears went in my coffeepot and turned into Bells, into owl feathers, into Rose petals, the likes of which I've never seen, into Ash, into cities that sorrowed with their people, who had not wanted to destroy the very air; who wept to see the fish belly up in all the rivers, and then the birds; who wept more when the animals passed on their poisons, their sicknesses, and sons and aunts began to die too, and the cities with them. What sorrow, it is best left buried, you might say. But a Juniper—why should she have to bear it alone in all her roots? A burden, it must be shared. We must share it.

And so, here they are. The dust-blue berries. Anja's Seven.

ONE

OH MAMA, JUNIPER MAMA, MY OWN WHEEL MAMA, I'VE BORNE NOT A baby but a pika. Seven actually, six girls, one boy, small as wild plums. I wanted so much for a baby that looked like Martin, with freckles and small pink hands. I wanted to be a normal strong woman and watch him learn to walk and stay here in the snow, circling their Road, teaching them the Ways of the Fools, and how to let the Wild Folk back in again. I wanted to be some kind of legend, I think, because I always felt like I was supposed to be one. I wanted to be the one to run through the melting spring and open each tree-door, let out the squirrel ladies with big tails for muffs and gambling nuts in their soft black coats. Surprise everyone. I'm a stupid girl, with pikas for her children. This was a completely different kind of surprise, and yet the People didn't seem to be surprised at all, which made it perhaps worse. I suppose I am arrogant, proud, taught to think I am someone special.

I wanted to paint over this place with my place and pretend that underneath there hadn't been any blood, nothing bad at all, that differences in history were unimportant. Everywhere there has been sadness; I just like not to look at it, to act as though these things don't change people, as though there is such a thing as a truly clean slate. My Wheel mama, she spoiled me. She kept me sheltered from the things she had suffered.

Let's just do it my way, I had come to say, and my Martin had followed me. I wanted to be like my mother, but maybe I didn't know what that really meant. My Martin had followed me across the big Valley with screams of buried rivers longing for flood in it. On top of them there were fields and fields once full of food so bountiful it could feed the world, but it was only bountiful because it was fed by poison, and that poison killed the ground and everybody nearby, eventually. As it always does. As we walked those fields were only dust at our ankles. The dust climbed up and with it the memory of the blood of the people there, at the End, fighting for that Food which was not life-giving at all, but had death in every seed.

I should have known up here, where the snow falls and melts and makes the water clear, at its beginning, that these People were not like us at all. In order to have survived, they had only up to run. Here, the highest of places, the harshest of places, where only the mercy of the wild could keep them alive.

I have tried to speak of my mother Wheel, of my aunt Ffion, of Iris, but these People here, they only smile politely, stir the stew, change the subject to next month, when the snows will begin to melt, when the walking will start up again.

My seven babies—I did not even know what they were when they came out clawing and whiskered. They mewled for me to wipe the placenta from their tiny dark noses. They are not creatures we have back in our place. Martin was right outside and he ran in at the end. He scooped those little ones toward me, sweet man, a better heart than I have, truly—golden. Mine is made of Pride. He didn't flinch. For a second, I thought of letting them smother. It's horrible. I, the daughter of a Buckeye, I should of all people be tolerant. I cry at night, knowing I had that thought. A hypocrite, I am. A bad woman, I am. My mama kept me too safe, too special, and thought that kindness would come with the package. Maybe it didn't.

They were like baby rabbits, but rounder, with mouse-sized ears. How they quivered, all pink. Of course that murderous thought passed. I heaved them up on my breast and cleaned them. I let them drink with their tiny piercing teeth. The midwife had wiped me dark with hare blood, making me long for the way trees give birth—clean, the slow growing of a seed, the stately procession of its blossoming and fruiting. Not this screaming, this blood everywhere, mostly from the young doe-hare. Her ears did calm me, laid against my belly like she could hear those babies coming on through.

Now I wonder if it was their doing, some sorcery, to turn my baby, Martin's baby, into some cousin of the hare. We had made the little life in me fierce and deep in one of those barren fields of dust, no longer able to bear that wasteland. We sank into each other like the two last fruits with all the sweetness of all the fruits of the world packed into them.

As we walked and my belly grew, I am certain I felt human feet kicking, not furred and clawed. So I wonder still if some metamorphosis occurred, some meddling, the mountain air turning whatever had been in my womb to soup, and then to something new.

The midwife screamed when she saw the pikas come out, but not really with shock. No, it looked to me like glee, like joy, like something she had waited for but hadn't been entirely sure would work out. She brought over another woman, and an old man who carried a battered instrument called a clarino. He played on it the saddest high song, a wail, with stars falling in it. My babies—pikas, the people kept murmuring, pikas!—huddled all around my neck as Martin ran his hands again and again through my hair and stroked their tiny pink backs with his big fingers which he could make so soft.

Extinct, they were saying—they've been dead since just after the Fall. World got too hot for them, with that thick fur. All dead. They were whispering, fast, not really to me at all. Is it really them? The midwife nodded, pleased, as if she herself had brought them into the world. Soon the whole encampment, bundled in their sturdy felts, in their tall fur caps, was huddled around that winter solstice hut-den where a stranger had birthed pikas. They all had small bells in their hands, and they were ringing them, a sweet cacophony.

I became a sort of oddity, a kind of pet. The pikas were what everyone had longed for, not me. I was like the river that bears the vessel full of an old friend thought lost at sea. No one cares at all about my own mother, the river that bore me, and all of us, up to high ground. I guess they are already on their own high ground, the highest, and have no need of our Way.

I miss her, my Wheel-mama, my axis. I wish she would tell me—Anja, sweetheart, my little buckeye-flower, here are blackberries for you, honey, the woodrats picked them, come, eat up, and what a big strong lady you'll become.

TWO

Two moons have passed and my pikas are already almost grown. What torture is this to a mother? They are little strangers, really—since the beginning they have been. Still, the dense chestnut of their fur, their long toes like hands, their black eyes that watch me softly and blink with happiness when I have been away and come back to them—these things have come to turn me tender. And I wonder, at night, cupped around Martin in the round tent they have given us—it seems they want us to stay, me the exceptional brood mare, Martin a good hand at chopping wood—where were they before? If they were all gone from the world, the last mothers and fathers expired in their winter dens in the talus, filled with their haystacks of grass, where were those little pika-seeds hiding? In the wind, and they drifted like dandelion propellers out over the Valley, slipped in me with Martin as we cradled and we crooned so desperately, full of sadness?

In a pocket of my mind, or maybe my heart, I know things. I know to teach my pikas to gather and to store certain grasses for winter, in tall haystacks, in dens of granite they are making now, that far in advance. It's like I've been turned a little bit pika myself. Just enough to show them by example, but not enough for us to speak. They are settling each into a territory, like we do, I suppose. I keep expecting one to shift, finally, to some round-eared girl—adorable, how I would kiss her apple-blossom cheeks!—and tell me to spin that haystack grass to gold, or find the needle of my death in it. Like our Wild Folk would have done. But such things don't happen here. People speak of black bears like cousins down the road, yellow-billed magpies like misbehaved brothers-in-law—but they all keep their dark feathers, their dark fur, and no words are exchanged that I have heard. No burly women amble up to the camp while the girls are having climbing competitions in the snowy cedars and demand that one be her companion, her house-maid, for a year and a day. No blue-jays require plates of shining glass, metal, blue plastic, to be left for them in tree crotches.

They don't want my thoughts on the subject—that much has not changed, not with these wanderers of their single circular Road. They loop around the Road yearly. The summit of the mountain at the center of it is topped with a glacier. That's the axis. On the Road we are moving toward meadows rich with seed, deer places, berry patches.

We are unmoored, my Martin and I. They seem to see us as their disciples. Quite the opposite of what we had expected, though Martin is demure. He watches the men trap squirrels with admiration. We could just walk down the mountain, and home. I know. But we don't. Maybe it's just the air, so thin and cold with the stories of snow in it. Or the blue peaks rough as teeth, glowing at dawn. Alpenglow, they call it, like the word is a bell being rung for a prayer. Or that they know pieces of this world that I don't. They hold them far under their furs and felts, pieces of the husking of this land, pieces of the source of All Water, All Rivers. I want to hold these pieces in my hands like the organs of the doe-leveret that were given to me to eat after I gave birth: heart, liver.

I am used to getting what I want, Martin tells me as he kisses my cheek and my neck, then all of me. I laugh, because this is true. Everybody and everything is not a mother, carrying to you handfuls of blackberries. I must learn to find, and to pick, my own. And so we will stay.

THREE

This time—only three months since the pikas, god save me—Martin and I have made two bighorn sheep lambs for babies. Their hooves and knees bruised my every corner coming out. Maybe it is the water here, the snowmelt. Maybe it has old ghosts stuck there, waiting to be swallowed down. Because at the sight of those rumpled brown bodies, hoofed, little noses fluttering, the midwife again yelled with joy but not surprise, and gestured over the old man with the clarino, who got teary eyed, again and again saying—"the sheep, the sheep have returned, the bighorn sheep!" He played a slow reel on his instrument, lilting, which made the ears of my little lambs perk and move. They were so much mine in that moment, covered still in the fluids from my body, more mine then they ever would be again.

I like to watch them leaping in the snow. They seem never to sink. Martin and I sit for hours this way, wrapped in many layers because the spring is only now thawing through the world. We hold hands. We don't speak. We behold them, close-curled brown fur, growing stubby horns, this brother and sister, as they leap from stone to stone as if there could be nothing at all more joyous in the world.

FOUR

We have been a year and a day on their Road. The whole circle, the whole circumambulation of that glacier which they call Beatrice Mother of Waters. A year and a day is a long time to be tested, to be held distant, to be treated only politely but never with tenderness. These are patient and hard people. Martin kept hold of my hand every day. We hung to each other and the babies at our ankles, gathering wood with the rest, making felt from rabbit fur.

They have a brood of rabbits, kept very safe and hidden, carried on a sort of litter which the men take turns hoisting on their shoulders, laughing—"our dozen Queens!" These rabbits have long fur, exceptionally so, and soft. I learned from the other women how to make felted coats and hats, mittens and slippers, from their wool. How to make a red dye from crushed cinnabar found only in one place, a ledge and a cavern reached around September, near the base of the glacier.

They acted, those women, like I spoke another language. And maybe, I have found, I did. I still do. My pika children, my big-horned lambs—these they seemed to understand and to take to more than I, though I have still yet to see or hear a word pass between them.

In that year I gave birth also to a grizzly bear cub, the color of honeycomb and granite dust, with teeth that scarred my nipples. Even she they would not let me mother as I wanted to—holding her always to me, bathing her tenderly in every blue stream, wreathing her in green braids of sweetgrass.

"She isn't all yours," they would say to me, passing the cub around in their arms, then leaving her in a meadow to find her way after us, to catch a ground squirrel on her own, discovering the strength of her jaws. I think I was always waiting, each time, for the little person to eventually unfurl from under that fur of bear, pika, sheep. I think they knew this, and would not let me rub off my humanness on them.

Now, we are back again, here. Where you are, your dark tunnel where I can chatter like a girl to her gossiping friend. A year and a day, sullen for much of it was I, even when they fawned over my summer shed hair, velvet green, and gave it all to my pikas for their new nests. None of my babies stayed with me. They are wild again already, having chosen each a place to live, to make their lives as grazers, as seed-gatherers, as rambling hunters, following me no further. Back where they belong, the women mutter. Back where they belong.

They have told us one new thing—a year on their Road for this, a hard apprenticeship, but I think their reserve has to do with trusting. Their world is made from the ashes of a harsh escape. They gave it to us like a special, rare berry, candied and glistening, as we sat all around the thickness of a second solstice fire, snow making the world drift soft and cold into its own dreaming.

"Under my skin, I change and I go out to meet them." A woman named Susannah said this right into my eyes, and Martin's. "Everything is at its source, here." She had hair the color of snow though she was only a little older than Martin. It matched, right then, the ground and the trees in the darkness, and so her face seemed to float before us.

"Oh," I said, not understanding. Martin only nodded. We did not have a clue what she meant, not really. We drank up the dark elderberry Winter Tea, for keeping sickness away, left in our cups. She didn't say anything else, only went back to a piece of rabbit felt in her lap and the pinwheels she was embroidering there.

I wanted to say—oh yes, you know, my mother is Wheel. She has wheeled feet, and rolls. But there is nobody here like my mother, or like any of the Fools, really—nobody torqued or numerous of limb, hair falling or round backed or with extra fingers, eyes, nipples. Holy strange ones, we were. Some of us normal in appearance, of course, by whatever standards approve such things, but soft in heart or mind somewhere, somehow, in some way that made that Old Way of ours, with the Masters and the Tool Sheds, unbearable. Once it was said a body or a mind got shaped thus from the poisons of Before—freaks and rubbish. But in my mother's tree-tent world, we were our own Court and every odd shape was a strength that said—I've been marked by the past of my species, yes, and by what was left behind, but it is no illness, no, it is a little doorway, my body, my mind, and tenderness lies on the other side. Tenderness, tenacity, teal-blue slippers for dancing on Wheel's webs and calling down the night-flying barn owls to wheel at our hands, a strange hybridity of woman and wild.

I wanted to tell Susannah all of this as she stitched that pinwheel shape in deer gut thread on the green of the rabbit felt—under *my* skin, there are many stories, I wanted to say. But I know she was making the Road, and the axis of Beatrice Mother of Waters, and the lines going there each a different month of the year—a calendar of walking. So I kept quiet, and wondered who it was she went out to meet, changing only under her skin.

FIVE

Five years, fifty little ones. I feel like a tree. I am half one, I must remind myself, bearing one glossy buckeye after another. All of them have been creatures these People call extinct. Their bloodlines lost. I wonder desperately where I have been storing them. Or if it is in Martin, from all his time underground by torch, brushing against myriad roots and bones. If he got seeded with lost ones down there.

I can tell you each species: pika, bighorn sheep, grizzly bear, yellow-legged frog, great gray owl, willow flycatcher, yellow-bellied marmot, Yosemite toad, even the seeds of a wooly sunflower. I feel more like a river bearing ships than a mother—each finding again its old berth, and my only purpose to get them there.

I've said it before: we could leave. We could walk back down this mountain, down from this cold. But they are kinder now to us, if only by a little, calling us by our names, smoothing at my hair when the next little seedling comes. That's what Martin and I call them now, what we murmur, laying together in the dark after making love. Who will it be, who are you, little seedling?

And what is it, we say together on early mornings, having tea inside the pale skin of our round tent, watching the kingfisher hunt across some clear alpine lake out the unrolled felt of our window—what is it beneath all of their eyes that keeps us here? What is it that spins them around and around this glacier, and us with them, like all the spokes on a Wheel?

Well, a person cannot very well *leave*, wanting the answer to such a question.

SIX

The glacier is the shape of a nipple, or a breast. When snow falls and then melts it is like milk in all the streams. All the streams go eventually to the rivers buried halfway in cement under the Valley. We walked together in what seems like a different life entirely, a different Anja, a different Martin, whose lungs had not yet been winnowed by alpine air, ice crystals, whose bodies had not yet become two floodgates. His into mine, mine into theirs, into hers, that peak, these mountains called the Sierra Nevada. If it is ever a human child, Martin, my love, I will call her Sierra, and if she has a brother, a twin, he will be Nevada, for here is the spine of the world and the snow its milk.

Here, the people seem first like this ice and this snow, cold and beautiful and impossible to hold, but it is only because they fled here. I have learned this. In all of them is the strength and the sadness of fleeing a land that maybe the world had once called the place of Milk and Honey, because fruits were grown there and sent on ships and airplanes to every corner of the earth. Yes, it was called this, the big long Valley we walked, only dusty now from its unnatural and poisoned fertility. When the World Fell, at the End, they have told us that a person had to flee, or fight, or die. Mostly all three at once. They have stories here around the fires about Demons. But I've learned this to be another word for a person who would kill you with any handy pipe, piece of car door or broken bottle, for the clothes on your back, for the last cans of your beans, for your pretty little daughter. Only people who could turn their hearts to ice, and climb the granite with their hands, having each lost someone they loved more than the sun itself, made it up here, and survived. Now there is nobody down there but ghosts.

They never had a Fool's Revolt of fire and webs. They never had a Lyoobov made out of Dreams. Only that fleeing—running away its own revolution, a form of new creation, of hope. Nobody made it up here but the strongest, the longest of limb or the most wiry and tough. I don't like to think of those buried along the way, but on the Road we say their names and throw down the petals of wild roses that the oldest women have saved. I did not know this for many years. The names are plants, because everybody changed them as they fled together, to leave behind that other time. Peony, Oak, Forget Me Not, Foxtail, Ryegrass, Tule, Milkmaid, Alder, Mint. Great-great-great grandmothers and grandfathers to the People whose Road we walk now. It was all so many generations ago but the people and their Road keep tight to their bones, they make like the snow, they speak still of the Fleeing, the Fires in the Valley, the Climbs, the Ones that Had to Be Left. The way we speak of the Fool's Revolt, and much longer before of Lyoobov, Rose, and Ash.

They say it has been three centuries of their walking that one peak called Beatrice. They say their walking has made the glacier stay alive, because when they arrived it was melting, and now it has stopped.

I know all these things because this winter—our eleventh, oh, time—I asked. I set down my pride at last at the foot of the glacier in October when we were nearest it, picking the last wildflower seeds in meadows above the treeline, running after the pikas that now teem amongst the talus rocks. My little furred great-grand children. I set down, forever, my Ambitions—you know the ones we've had to Teach, to be Models. I asked—who are you? How did you come to be here?

To my great alarm, all the men began to weep, and the women soothed them with strong hands on their backs. I learned that they kept tallies, in their memories, of every creature lost across the centuries. Every one extinct. Every one gone. And they walked to keep the glacier from melting. And they walked to mend what they called the Hole in the Sky Which is in Each of Us. We have kept the waters going, they told us. We have held the sky up. We have kept the names of all the wild ones who have come and gone—

"Wild Ones! Oh, yes—" I began to say, I began with the egret women, the squirrel ladies, my buckeye father, my spider grandfather, on my tongue.

"No," the women said to me, straightening their fur and felt hats, rubbing their noses at the cold. "No."

"It is *we* who go to meet *them*, in their skins," said Susannah, for the second time in a decade. Susannah was always the kindest to us. "It was the only way to survive, for our First People. Learn to be like the coyote as she hunts voles. Learn to find sweet roots like the brush rabbit and the ground squirrel. Learn to make a home like the woodrat and the magpie. Learn to move on, and move on, and move on, like the black bear. Our side of the world was too ravaged by the poisons that drifted from your Cities, over your Bay and up our Rivers, for there to be any women with the faces of foxes to reach out their womanly hands and hold ours. Under our skins we each must learn the Way of one creature. I the newt. She the deermouse. He the gray fox. He the crow. That is how we can carry on, year by year, and let the Terror Known in that Valley slide away and evaporate. That is how we have learned again of all the mountain food. That is how we have kept the Hole from opening more, the Glacier from melting. We've gone to the middle to meet them. Reached out a hand like this—" the midwife reached her hand to Martin as Susannah spoke. "—said I am Susannah. I need you. I need to be part of your family or I will die. I need to be forgiven. Will you forgive me? Will you forgive us? And then you sit down in the dirt, and you wait, maybe for three whole days, until an animal walks by. He is your brother. He is the one you will learn from. You will call him brother. You will not be so needy or so weak as to make him turn from skunk into a man in order to understand each other. Beneath your skin, you make your soul grow black and white fur, you learn to let off that smell, you give him your hand. You are his brother. This is what we are made for. We tell stories and become new creatures. A skunk, he is a skunk, purely."

SEVEN

To walk the Road around Beatrice Mother of Waters is a worship.

Martin is the one of the two of us who finally found the way in. He learned before me what it is that keeps them, and therefore us, circling, circling, walking that Road close to the bone of the mountain, like homing birds, like if we stopped the sky would fall all blue on our heads. A joyful walking it is. We carry the long-haired rabbits now in boxes with wheels that seven big-horned sheep pull along with us. Each month we gather different wild herbs to keep us strong—yerba santa, sagebrush, yarrow, o'shalla root, manzanita leaves, mountain sorrel. We are learning to wheel just like the stars know how to wheel, lighting fires each night.

Nineteen years on this Road now it's been, wheeling, dropping little flycatcher chicks, golden beavers, kit foxes, like buckeyes, along the way. I have learned to relax and give birth like a tree. It took that long to learn to see what it is they see, what it is they know.

One morning, in mid-June, we were passing my favorite place, a flat high meadow above the trees, just granite, grass, a still lake, snow still on the ground. Martin saw the men moving off to go hunting for deer. They'd never invited him because he had Too Many Thoughts, apparently. That's what they told him. Loud Thoughts. This time, he looked up and saw them going, and in the dawn before his eyes they had short tails and the shadows of antlers. Not props or decoys, but real, like learning to see all over again, Martin told me. He followed them, quiet as a mole in the underground.

I think now that they *chose* to show him their deer tails and their antlers that morning as we woke, stretched, washed our socks in the lake and touched one another's cheeks over a breakfast of sheep's milk, pinyon pine nuts and alpine strawberries. I think they knew that he followed, and wanted him to. Nineteen years—now *that* is a truly long apprenticeship. The moon is again amidst the stars of the Northern Crown, like the first summer we walked their Road.

The men did not go hunting at all. They went straight up the peak of Beatrice Mother of Waters, climbing on black hooves, even though they stood up like men. Martin hung back, and from a distance it was impossible after a while for him to tell what parts were man, what deer, or if, after all, there were stags among them too—and had there been all along?

They went straight up and in. Yes, right into that glacier. Big cold tunnels narrow as a man's shoulders, blue with icicles, creaking and singing their ice songs, my Martin told me. When he told me he wept for what he had seen, for what he had heard, that glacier creaking and moaning all around him the ice-melodies of its old, cloud-made heart. Down under the ice there were tunnels and cavern soft granite. Dripping slick places. The antlers of those men glowed along the way and my Martin knew how to follow, feeling with his hands and knees, lost in a dizzy place where he was nine years old again and following the glowing tails of Seven Hares, his only friend the Handless Fool, the bones of Frances and his Chinook ash-smudged in his backpack. He told me he was that boy for a timeless crawling span, eyes wet with fear and longing, for his father, who he never saw again. It was as if time itself had collapsed around him in that peak, below its glacial breast of snowmelt. Eyes full of the memory of the fire where Frances and his Chinook were burned—that single miracle, that final Salmon, that final Saint.

The tunnels widened into one cave. Huge, my Martin told me, some great hall or cathedral of stone, neither of which we'd ever seen but had imagined. Bigger than my mother's Court of Webs. The walls were covered in red and black paintings of animals. A dance of them. Herds, circling the walls, shifting by the light of the candles the hunters lit, the wicks of juniper fuse lanterns. Amidst all the animals, Martin saw the big-wheeled beast of all the old stories, Lyoobov. Trunked, graceful, wide. He cried aloud, but no one looked back at the place where he hid.

The men were beginning their own dance. Martin said that first it looked like a hunt—arms thrusting and parrying, as if with spears or arrows, then a frenzied closeness of bodies. Stag, man, doe, like some vast and illuminated lovemaking. The air got thick, ghost-filled, shadows of salmon flickering on the ceiling, wolverine and red fox, willow flycatchers, condors, goshawks, fishers and yellow legged frogs. Shadows of martens, bighorn sheep, flickering newts and woodpeckers and spotted owls, grizzly bears. One man played a strange, small bone instrument against his teeth that created a humming and a twanging so strange it shook Martin in his blood. The other men chanted, in harmonies, layered and lilting, these words: olive-sided flycatcher, great gray owl, black backed woodpecker, pika, marten, wolverine, coho, Chinook, yellow-back marmot, Yosemite toad, foxtail pine, incense cedar, California nutmeg, wooly sunflower. And on, and on. My children were in those names, and many more. Ones who were or had been extinct from the world, culled.

As the chanting and the twanging quieted, the men became all-the-way bucks. They began to lick at the walls, as if for salt. One man remained a man, and he said, as if he wanted Martin to hear, though no one so much as glanced toward the place where he crouched: "We are all the Animals Under Our Skins. We are the Wild Folk. It is a matter of dreaming into your cave heart, and calling up the one who is ready to return. Willow flycatcher. Ice. Chinook. Lady of Rivers. It may take a long, long time."

I gave birth to a clutch of tiny eggs three days later. Willow flycatchers, they all crooned, touching my belly, looking at their glacier, unsurprised.

And so it is simple, this act of being forgiven. As simple as giving your hand to a lover, and as terrifying, saying—I leave my heart here, underground, with yours. It was never mine, was it, but yours?

ALL AT ONCE THE JUNIPER, WITH ANJA IN HER, WAS FINISHED. OUR cups empty. We both sat in the smoke of the fire as it hissed to embers.

"Do you know what it is to be heartbroken?" said that old dusty woman, folding her dozen arms into a knot. I, with tears all down my face, only laughed.

"The only other piece I can tell you, the only one I can pull out of all these rings of mine like a gold wedding band from Before, is this. It is said here, whispered by the dead bodies of the fish who rotted and were eaten by bears, who excreted them at my roots and fed me, that Martin found, under his skin, the Chinook he'd always sought. One morning when Anja woke up he was gone, not beside her. Instead of him the streams were thick with spawning Chinook, all red and silver, egg-laying, dying. He was one of them. He didn't know it would be so easy, and he also didn't know he would never hold his Anja again. It is said that amidst all those fish was a small man, Frances, on a wooden Chinook, and it is said the grizzlies who had grown up, who had once been the Children of Anja and Martin, they gathered at the banks, growling up some ancient glee. This, their favorite worship, their favorite dance: to eat the salmon all along the banks, expired from their final loving. It is said that Frances and his wooden Chinook were swallowed whole, and maybe Martin too, after those first bright red eggs in a lifetime were laid.

"And it is said that Anja could not live without her Martin, her last, first and only friend. If you were to look, you'd find a single, impossible buckeye, huge and broad-hipped, growing at the base of the glacier called Beatrice Mother of Waters. Against all odds, all laws, with her roots in ice which some say is really the Milk of the World. Every year though, that buckeye loses her leaves, then drops her glossy nuts, then regrows her leaves and the intoxicating spires of her flowers. When she drops those buckeye nuts in the thousands across the stone, the ice, they roll down to the alpine fields. I could not tell you what is inside each nut, for they cannot be leeched and pounded like normal buckeyes. Some say they are the Fertility of the World, and when you bury them, Lost Things grow there—languages, songs, sage species, passerines. Her roots grow down into a cave, that cave, where People learned again that they are Animals, and must reach out their hands."

The old Juniper woman looked tired. She grew sad, and I saw all at once that the smoke had grown because her dry bark was on fire above us, a dark smolder. I jumped up. I yelled out. I began to run for water. The smoke thickened in my eyes, but I saw a last glimpse of her, smiling, serene, sad, dozen-armed, the colors of her berries, fading slowly into the bark.

The fire was enormous. I, small Poppy, screamed out like the little pikas, the bears, the woodpeckers—Anja's great, great, great a dozen times grandchildren, I suppose—who'd come to see. In the end only a big pile of embers remained, and the whole Camp, led by Sare, stood behind me, staring.

It was Lyoobov who made it all right. She rolled up. She put the embers one by one into her mouth, below her gentle trunk, grunting softly. Sare held my hand but did not say, "What have you done?" She seemed melancholy, but not mad.

We all watched Lyoobov eating the embers of the juniper tree where Anja had tucked her Seven Memories, where all the stories of Before, and Fools, and Wild Folk, had gathered in constellations, hypnotized. They glowed as they went down her throat. She grew hot as a bonfire. Sare's people smiled at each other from beneath their tall fur hats. I felt sad, remembering that old dusty lady, the sound of her voice, the cups we shared.

"Do you walk the Road?" I whispered to her, not wanting her to ever let go of me. She nodded.

"Yes, yes, and underneath I am Ursa, and in our walking we keep the waters clean. Did you ever wonder? We are a giant Water Wheel, a giant Wheel where the animals can again come from the places they hid, and trust that in the world they again have brothers and sisters. They are not alone. We remember their names as precious as our names. Sare. Poppy. Black bear, gray fox. My heart—it's bear-swallowed, see?"

I could only nod, and gulp, and grow red in the face.

"Nobody expected you'd be so little and odd," Sare whispered to me. "It's been such a long time, waiting, for the one to thread the needle and stitch the mountains back to sea, make the Road for the Animals and the Waters again. They've been so scared, see, thinking you won't know them, thinking you'll do what you've always done."

That afternoon, we sat around the last smolder of the juniper and cooked rabbits for lunch. I put a few final embers and ash, mixed with water, in my coffeepot, and let it simmer, then poured everyone a cup. They chuckled, thinking I was mad and pouring them wet, dirty tree pulp. Out came something pure white and steaming. They lifted wooden cups to their lips with shock and drank. Sweet milk, juniper or rosemary or sage spiced, maybe all of those flavors together. None of us could decide. We closed our eyes as we sipped.

"Some change is coming," said Sare's father, who had been smoking the fish when we arrived. He took a long gulp and eyed me, not unkindly.

"Can I keep this?" Sare murmured to me, pulling the little goldfinch from her many ragged skirts—skins, red nettle fabric, yellow dyed rabbit wool. Inside, the map was different. Now it led in white lines like milk, from that glacier-peak, Beatrice Mother of Waters, to our Bay. "In case I ever wanted to visit."

I didn't even know what to say. I got a big lump in my throat and tried not to cry. "Nobody's ever been nuts enough to do such a thing, to leave our safety here, but maybe that will change," she continued, taking my silence for a yes. She did not know that what I wanted to say was—*I would stay here forever if you'd be my friend, always. Nobody, no person, has ever looked me in the eye and seen me there.* Or maybe she did know that. She had yellow eyes like a bear, and her skin dark as pine bark, and she grinned.

We left the next morning. I wanted to stay. I wanted to walk their Road dressed in furs, and hold Sare's hand, and see the buckeye growing at the base of the glacier. I wanted to remain amidst that spare peace. I wanted to see Anja. Lyoobov, though, she told me you can't always get things just the way you want them. She knew something that she wouldn't tell me, and so did everyone else. She pushed me along. I left weeping just like a child on her back, which was warm from all those embers. Sare gave me one perfect buckeye in exchange for the goldfinch. I knew it was Anja's. I carried it like a star fallen to earth in my pocket, wondering what it might grow. My hands were dark-smudged with juniper ash and chapped with cold.

The air got thick again as we descended, rolling, to that dead Valley, which Anja had wept for in all of her Seven. Dust, cement, scraps of ghost-house and steel. That Valley which had made the People flee, and throw their arms into the ice and the cold peak.

You will not believe it when I tell you the next part. The last part. Not until you see it with your own eyes, not until you go to the Bay and the Straits and see it coming, all froth and sediment.

When we reached that big Valley it was night again. Stars made their milky river overhead. I thought of all the stories, those ghosts with starry edges. I climbed down and into the trapdoor of Lyoobov's belly to sleep, thinking

I would sweat all night with the heat. I was looking forward to it, to the feeling of my whole body crying out its salt and with it my sadness at leaving that place pure as the snow peak, where people were odd and fox-swallowed, like me.

Inside, I found that Lyoobov was full of bells the color of embers, warm to the touch but not painful. Round and fluted bells, big as my head or bigger. They were not perfect and glossy but cracked, re-soldered, lined, like they had seen the Beginning, the Middle and the End of the World As It Was Before, and had come out again the other side. Cracked, re-stitched. Like all of us still here. I took a bell in each hand and rang them together, gently. The sound broke my heart like it was nothing but a leaf, torn to tatters. The sound ran through me like blue river water, like a mother's milk, like the first time I saw Lyoobov and put my hand to her skin, like the night when it falls, like the flight of owls, like the memory of my human mother, my Molly, and Sam sitting by me with a fishing pole, not knowing how to speak to me, nor I to him.

Lyoobov started to make a strange sound, a purring. It rumbled. I heard something enormous crack, heave and sing the way you imagine planets singing up there in the spheres. The ground was moving. I rang more bells, unable to stop myself, intoxicated with the sound, exhilarated that it seemed to be shaking the very earth. The cracking grew louder, and Lyoobov's purring did too, and then a rushing began, just like water. I felt afraid but couldn't stop that ringing. I went round and round ringing those bells, one by one.

My head seared with their reverberations, and my chest did too, until I wondered if my heart was also a bell, eagerly clinking and echoing. When I could bear it no longer, I slipped out of Lyoobov and saw what had happened.

The Rivers were coming all at once. Welling up, breaking the asphalt, sending up clouds of dust, then swallowing them. I climbed to the top of Lyoobov's back, which vibrated like she was all one bell, and then the waters came and engulfed us. I screamed. I did not want to drown. Lyoobov, she looked at me gently, and bobbed upward.

We floated.

Before my eyes, like some oceanic tide, the Valley filled with those two rivers called the Sacramento and the San Joaquin. Sacrament and Saint. As they came up from the ground, I thought for a moment that I saw two figures, a man and a woman, pulling the Rivers behind them, tearing open the ground, each wreathed in sedges and tules, mud-smeared, blue. Then, nothing, just that great flooding. Dams, I think, were shattering everywhere all through the foothills, and they made a din too. It was an angry and an eager flooding, and we floated on that great lake, that inland ocean. The very dirt below seemed to groan and croon with pleasure.

This is the part you will believe the least. The water, well, it wasn't water at first, but milk. I swear to you upon my fox-swallowed and Molly-made heart, it was milk. The milk of every mammal come and gone. The milk that is the dust between stars. The milky sap of plants.

I looked back at the mountains from where we'd come and saw that the peak Anja had called Beatrice Mother of Waters was no longer a white cap on top of a ridge, with granite sharp and dark below it; the glacier was streaming, turning the hole mountain white. Not melting, it seemed to me, but erupting.

Swarms of honeybees materialized with the dawn and hummed around us, everywhere, lapping at the river-milk, dropping the yellow pollen from their legs. By midday the milk was golden with pollen. Lyoobov and I floated in a daze, drinking the milk dusted with pollen, which tasted sweet and sour and buttery at once.

For months, Lyoobov and I floated through that Valley full of milk. Miles and miles we floated with the currents, heading west. We left Sare and her People in early winter, and floated for a whole season in milk. By late spring it was all gone, beneath us only normal river water, murky green-brown with sediment and those centuries underground. Maybe it all got lapped up by the dry land below, or maybe just mixed in with the water as it began to run clear. Like a wound, cleaning itself. We floated, dreaming. Not thinking much at all because, you see, we felt such calm, though we didn't know, really, if this meant the world had ended again, or was just beginning.

After those months drinking milk and honey, we reached the delta that opens through the Strait and into the Bay. By then all the waters had lowered and we floated on a normal river, no milk, no inland sea. The water flowed by with pieces of broken cement, block after block, getting rid of it all.

We climbed onto the shore, reluctantly, like getting out of bed after a long dream. Cold feet to the dirt. But it was good like that too—the feeling of stretching, taking in gulps of air, feeling the sunlight as if brand new.

As we began the last bit, rolling up and down, up and down, the three ridges and three valleys, toward home, here among the meadows and the alders near the ocean, we looked back once. A woman was coming behind us. Far behind, a mile or two, but in that flat expanse of delta and empty hills, we could see her and hear the clatter of hooves, the padding of paws, the flapping of wings, behind her. She had a huge dark coil of green hair, and the wind blowing from the east brought us the smell of rosemary. Behind her walked flocks of pronghorn antelope and tule elk, yellow legged frogs, grizzly bears and golden beavers, in some kind of peaceable truce together. Above flew spotted owls, night herons, a bald eagle, tiny brown wrens. A single barn owl with big yellow eyes, the one who is with us still—she flew right toward us, and landed like home on Lyoobov's back.

The woman with green coils of hair walked beside a big tawny cow with black eyes who wore a bell on her neck that clanked. Milk dripped from hooves and talons and paws as they mounted one of the old roads that led west, the same one we used, a wide highway grown thick with dandelions. They dripped milk like they'd waded knee-deep in the stuff. She waved at me like she knew me, then shooed me on with her hands.

So here I am. Before you. This is all I Know.

POPPY WAS FINISHED. HE SHUT LYOOBOV'S BOOK. THE RAVENS HAD flown close, because they knew a good thing when they heard it. Everyone was so deep-fallen into Poppy's words, they did not notice the multitudes of antelope, of tule elk, the myriad yellow legged frogs, the quiet clans of grizzly bears, and behind Molly, the most beautiful woman you could imagine, dark hair a fragrant coil, a green fringe at the backs of her hands, holding a Jersey cow on a nettle rope, amidst them all, listening.

Slowly, Poppy walked to Lyoobov's belly and climbed inside. The barn owl with great yellow eyes followed. They both came out bearing armloads and talons-full of big bells. Poppy carried the single buckeye seed in his shirt. Then he began to ring the bells, one by one, while the barn owl circled, and everybody's heart broke right in two, like nuts split in half to let their tendriled stalks begin to grow.

By way of an Afterword

SINCE BEFORE I COULD UTTER WORDS, I THINK I HAVE ALWAYS SEEN around the corners of things. As a child this could sometimes be unsettling, but over the years of becoming the artist that I had no choice but to be, I learned that I could paint these folk I saw or dreamed or felt, these otherwhere places which seemed at once familiar and strange, and that painting was a kind of language in which I could sing invisible threads between things. These days I describe my paintings as *Waymarkers to the Otherworlds* because I am fascinated by the shamanic process inherent in creating art, and the way a powerfully wrought image really can take you to another place, and cause tangible change.

My work conjures a kind of folktale world, though the paintings are mostly not illustrations of actual stories. The people and landscapes and objects and atmospheres I create are from some kind of peasant-fable, situated perhaps somewhere between Russia, Finland and Northern Germany / Poland; it's a timeless place that I think corresponds to a kind of Old Europe, but really cannot be pinned on a map or historical timeline. People often comment that my paintings are sad, which I suppose in a way they are, though to me it is a beautiful melancholy, a yearning ache: I am painting in a minor key. But most of all, people ask me to tell them the stories behind my paintings, and I can never give them an answer because the stories woven inside my works are different for every person who steps toward them, and often I do not know how they begin or end myself.

So, imagine my delight when I received stories written for my paintings by someone else! Sylvia Linsteadt began at first using my images as inspirations, as starting blocks to initiate pieces of writing, but upon embarking on this creative journey, found that the union of our worlds opened up a whole new one and that the words just tumbled out. I nervously read her first piece, written for *Lyoobov*—a piece I painted aged 18—and was totally shaken by the wonder and quality of her storytelling. She began writing more pieces to other paintings of mine and sent them to me, one by one. It was a strange and beautiful experience, getting to walk the forest glades of my own imagination and see them through the eyes of another; it was like being taken by the hand to a place you know well but which has changed since you were last there, and told all about it in words that ring familiar and yet new in your ears. Sylvia and I share many loves—for wilderness and otherness and for the odd and ragged characters and creatures that populate the edges of things, as well as an anger at the loss and destruction of land and old ways that we endure in this Twenty First Century. And so it makes perfect sense that we should combine our arts; but reading the tales of characters born from my own inner world was intimate and moving in a strange and unfamiliar way, and utterly delightful.

Gradually, as the stories grew in number, threads began to be woven between them, and the semblance of a mosaic story-cloth took shape. The tales ended up spanning many lifetimes, and are set in a mythic version of Northern California. The cycle of stories make up a post-apocalyptic folktale peopled with fools and wheeled creatures and storytellers and vagabonds and wise animal-women; how could I fail to be enchanted (in its truest sense—to be sung in by bewitchment)? These are the Otherworlds I spend most of my time in, painted in jewelled language, embroidered, re-mapped, lit up by Sylvia's exquisite and unique art, and I am honoured beyond words.

It is illustration turned on its head: in an appropriate upturning of the linear right-/left-brain order of things, the writing comes *after* the image, not before. In such a revolution, we are enabled once again to re-track those old once-known paths to the worlds beyond this one; this story has its roots in the magical earth of intuition because it came from the art. I believe this lends *Tatterdemalion* an unusual power: it is a story created by women in an upside-down way, celebrating the oddest and most marginal of characters and ways, and is utterly unhesitant about re-imagining an *uncivilisation*—ancient, wild and once more acquainted with the Dreaming.

May the integrity and true magic woven into these storied tatters sing open for you the vagabonding tracks to a new kind of wonder and bless your eyes and ears and hearts with the ointments of be*wild*erment.

RIMA

THE FIRST TIME I SAW ONE OF RIMA'S PAINTINGS, I EXPERIENCED A feeling of deep, animal resonance somewhere near my solar plexus. It was a startling bloom of recognition that felt like the opening of a brambled door I'd always carried in me, but had yet to discover until that moment. It was a feeling of utter joy. But it had about it a tremble of the uncanny too, the sort of tremble that makes you pause and wonder if there are places of pilgrimage to which many human imaginations may journey—common ground, like the ancestral spawning pools of Chinook salmon, the ancient calving thickets of caribou, the primordial nesting tundras of the wayfaring arctic tern. Seeing Rima's work opened the brambled door to an old footpath I'd been looking for in all my life's word-makings, probably since the age of seven when I one day lifted my pencil and decided I wanted to write tales. Until I glimpsed Rima's artwork, all the dusky-footed woodrat nests and gray fox dens I'd wandered through, the elk trails and bumble-bee flight paths, could never quite lead me there, to that particular door of thorn and dusty old sun and a doorknob of hedgehog vertebrae. Reaching it some two and a half years ago made me want to cry.

I can't remember now which painting I first glimpsed in Rima's Hermitage, which creation it was that flapped its strange, bloodred wings and revealed, on the undersides, the map to that storied place in my own mind which had been waiting, twiddling its thumbs, for me to find it. Maybe this is more illustrative than being able to point to a single one of Rima's works as some kind of sourcepoint in my memory—all of her creations, it feels to me, emerge from the same vast, strange, fierce landscape at once utterly wild and utterly tender, a place east of the moon, west of the present, and rooted deep in some fiddle-sung, bear-danced, rug-woven, mountain-path-caravan-trundled dirt. The eyes of her edgewalking people, her edgewalking animals and weeds and musical instruments, are lonesome, loving and wise, and they looked right into my bones and sang a song there that left me literally reeling and giddy for days.

As for *Tatterdemalion*, this ragged-kind creation with its skirts on backwards, a tophat of woodrat-palace sticks and a heart all milk and honey and tooth—it is, to date, the most joyous piece of writing I've made with these two hands (the one that holds the fountain pen, the one that steadies and smoothes the page). It was more like setting off on a strange new footpath in old, trusted boots, and seeing who next I met around the corner, than the usual feeling of coaxing people and animal and story from the mysterious soil (or sky) of the mind-heart-hand, where tales, for me, are normally found. With *Tatterdemalion*, I walked a while; I stopped for a cup of smoky tea on a piece of driftwood; I watched Ffion emerge from a bottle in the middle of a sea lion and introduce herself; I carried on. I met Anja at a crossroads, juggling buckeyes; she told me her tale and pointed the way to Lyoobov. And on it went, from a feral future San Francisco Bay (and more specifically West Marin) to the Sierra Nevada mountains and back, tracing the snow melt rivers to the ocean again by foot and paw and wheel. This is a strange patchwork cape of a tale told tattered, told true.

Literally, *Tatterdemalion* was born one day in the autumn of 2012, while sitting in my studio at the time (the old laundry-room-turned-back-door-landing of my brother's house in Berkeley, which smelled of some ancient detergent and flooded with the winter rains), staring at the wall and feeling that black doom of writer's block. Idly, I thought I might loosen up my imagination by writing something inspired by one of Rima's paintings. "Lyoobov" trundled through, and hitched my hands to his wheels and strange trunk. The woman and man on his back broke my heart, and the first piece in this book came pouring out. I sent it to Rima, thinking she might enjoy this front-to-back creation—a tale illustrating her painting with words. I wrote another ("Hark, Hark!") and another ("A Girl Mad as Birds"), and sent them all, rather surprised at what was coming out, at the wild familiarity of it all within myself. Rima suggested they'd make a nice book, and perhaps I should keep going? Why, yes! Suddenly, the characters were not disparate folk, but players in the same tale, startling me with the ways they wandered in, already knowing one another. But of course they did, didn't they, for they had all wandered into Rima's wildly fecund mind and hands first, calling out their greetings. She is the original alchemist who sang them down from the strangest of stars and up from the sweetest of root-tangles under the ground.

Tatterdemalion is thus a series of Rima's paintings that birthed a series of my own stories illustrating those paintings with words, back-to-front of the usual order of things. Rima's creations are whole worlds unto themselves, which brings me to my last and most important point of all—if these paintings are like the axles at the centers of myriad wheels (all bone and sinew and oak and metal flute scrap), then the stories I have written are single *spokes.* This is what makes Rima's work so especially beautiful: each painting is an endless world, a rainstorm of possible tales, a moment in time that might lead backward or forward in millions of possible directions. My tales are merely single drops. There is room for all of our stories inside the weedy seams of Rima's work. Bless her a hundred times over for this, and for the doorway she hitches open in every wild heart.

SYLVIA

Appendix of Rima Staines' Paintings

Titles in order of appearance

THE COFFEEPOT
A GIRL MAD AS BIRDS
LYOOBOV
HARK HARK
THE BELLS
SLOVA SOVA
LEG WHEEL AND JAW HARP
THE FISH EGG
WITCH BOTTLE
ANJA IN THE HORSE CHESTNUT
THE VISITORS
KAKUARSHUK
WAYFARER'S NATIVITY
SNOWFLIGHT UNDER THE SEASKY

ACKNOWLEDGEMENTS

MANY THANKS TO RIMA, OF COURSE, FOR HER ENDLESS, WISE INSPIRATION and pathmaking as an artist and friend; to my wonderful agent Jessica Woollard for her dedication, belief and vision and her support every step of the way; to the brilliant Jay Griffiths for first winging this book out into the world; to John Mitchinson for remembering and believing, and for breathing it all to life; to my editor Liz Garner, for her love of true old magic and her care and skill with words and myths and language-spells; to the wonderful team at Unbound, whose support and care and kindness made *Tatterdemalion*'s birth a thing of ease and bounty; to every person whose name is listed in the back of this book, for literally bringing it into the world, for making *Tatterdemalion* a community; to my family, for believing in my love of words and old worlds and strange enchantments from the very beginning; to my love, for always; and to the land of California and the stories in my blood, for saying *tell.*

SYLVIA

MY BIGGEST THANKS GO TO THE BEINGS WHO TOOK MY HAND EARLY on and bade me paint. But without the humans who came after, I wouldn't still be doing so. So, deep gratitude to my parents Pamela and James Staines who raised me surrounded by beautiful art-making, and instilled in me a belief that this soul-work was a valid path to take in life. Ongoing, wide-reaching gratitude to my beloved Tom Hirons who is pen to my paintbrush, supports me endlessly to create more, and who weaves with me the art and stories to come, not least of these—our beloved Orin, who scintillated my world a thousand-thousandfold when he came through and to whom it will all be passed on.

For seeing the stories in my art I must also thank the incredible Jay Griffiths whose belief in my work means a great deal indeed. I thank and salute John Mitchinson, Unbound's team and wide community of supporters for enabling such unusual and strange work to be published.

And most of all I must thank Sylvia—for she alone of all the people who look at my paintings and ask "What is the story behind it?" went behind to look, and came back with the most truthfully-enchanted story I have ever read.

RIMA

UNBOUND is the world's first crowdfunding publisher, established in 2011.

We believe that wonderful things can happen when you clear a path for people who share a passion. That's why we've built a platform that brings together readers and authors to crowdfund books they believe in – and give fresh ideas that don't fit the traditional mould the chance they deserve.

This book is in your hands because readers made it possible. Everyone who pledged their support is listed below. Join them by visiting unbound.com and supporting a book today.

David Abram
Debby Accuardi
Peter Adams
Caspar Addyman
Paul Agricola
Melanie Ainsbury-Dovey
Buket Akgün
Adrienne Alanis
Fern Leigh Albert
Robert Alcock
Jere Alexander
Marie Alftin
Per Alftin
Nina Allan
Carter Allen
Jenn Allen
Rebecca Altman
Jeanne Applegate
Maria Arambula
Suzanne Arnold
Xyara Asplen
Elizabeth Atwood
Jasmine Auerswald
Lesley Austin
James Aylett
Frances Bacon
Lindsey Bagnaschi
Amina Bahrami
Dana Bailey
Davina Balvack
Susanne Barker
Fiona Barnes
Alison Barry
Sally Basile
Sheila Batchelor
Gail Battaglia
Anna Bear
Kiri Bear
Beca Beeby

Francesca Bell
Lillian Bell
Devauges Benjamin
Madalyn Berg
Terry Bergin
Julia Bernardini
John Bevan
Keary Birch
Sharon Blackie
Christian Blanc
Lisa Blinn
Larry Blount
Joanne Blythe
Amy Bogard
Tarquin Bolton
Velma Bolyard
Robin Bond
Carrie Boon
Joan V Boos
John Boos
John D Boos
Julia Booth
Cindi Borax
David Borthwick
Martine Bos
Heidi Botes
Caroline Bowen
Sharon and Gavin Boyd
Phil Brachi
Kirsten Bradley
Jane Brant
Eliza Bratton
Richard W H Bray
Barbara Brayfield
Heather Brereton
Pete Briger
Jay Brightwater
Caroline Brindle
Jules Bristow
Kalanina Britton
Heidi Brooks
Angela Brown
Barbara Brown
Bonnie Brown
Marion Brown
Melanie Brown
Tess Bryant
Dana Bubulj
Gareth Buchaillard-Davies
Anne Buchanan
Meredith Buck
Mincka Buijs
Andrea Bukiewicz
Natasha Burge
Fran Burkell
Bernard Burns
Chuck Burr
Susan Burson
Alison Burton
Rebecca Burton
Beatrice Burwell
Molly Bush
Deborah Byrd
Christina Cairns
Bettina Calverley-Rowland
Jill Cansell
Nicola Capes
Elsinore Carabetta
Susi Carlson
To Carol
Melissa Carr
Marie Carson
Susan Cassidy
Dee Dee Chainey
David Lars Chamberlain
Shaun Chamberlin
Caroline Champin
Gaynor Chapman
John Luke Chapman
April Chase
Joy Cherkaoui
Patricia Cheyne
Sam Chittenden
ChloeOpal
Cathi Christmus
Elisheva Cieslewitz
James Clapp
Emma Clark
Katharine Clark
Rebecca Clark
Sarah Clarkson
Jane Clelland
Candice Collins
Kaylie Tyne Collins
Mariko Conner
Philip Connor

Courtney Cooke
Catherine Cooper
Lee Cope
Kaelee Corcoran
Tyler Cornelius
Julie Cottrell
Adam Court
Judith Craig
Kendal Craig
Alex Crane
Carla Crane
Suzi Crockford
Iris Croll
Jim Cummings
Diana Cunningham
Ola Czajkowski
Gail Davidson
Scott Davidson
Tiffany Davidson
Wendy Davidson
Sally Ann (Annie) Davies
Shelly Davis
Susan Davis
Jonathan Davison
Rosalee de la Foret
Claire Dean
Valerie Dean
Sarah Dearling
Erin Delsol
Angela DeMatteo
Harriet DeMoia
Julie Denning
Dorothea Deppe
John Detwiler
Jon Dick
Angela Dickson
Babac and Nancy Doane
Kimberly Dobrosky
Marylou Doherty
Therese Doherty
Linda Doughty
Rachel Dowse
Warren Draper
Mark Drummond
Amy Dunnigan
Vivienne Dunstan
Nicole Dupuis
Alys Earl
Terrie Ann Easley
Jolie Elan
Shannon Elkins
Brian Ellis
Matt Elphick
Rebecca Engen
Ali English
T. Erickson
Catherine Evans-Jones
Cate Jerle Fagan
Colleen Fagan
The family from The Land of Green Ginger
Issy Fandango
Adrian Farrel
Lyla Ray Fazey
Michael Fenwick
Andrea Ferrante
Cari Ferraro
Emma Finn
Anna Fisk
Susan Flynn
Abigail Folk
Folklings
Anna Forss
Bev Fox
Terri Francik
Cassidy Franklin-Dutton
Laura Fraser
Erin Frasheski
Kristin Frasheski
Megan Frasheski
Sophie Frederickson
Anna French
Susan Frentzos
Rachel Frigot
Patricia Frisch
Deborah French Frisher
Raquel Galindo
Hilary Gallo
Meghan Gemma
Georgina & Isi
Kim Gilligan
Donna Godfrey-Conyers
Ulric "Gestumblindi" Goding
Pilar Aceves Goeders
Kate Gold
Steve Golemboski-Byrne

Johanna Good
Mary Good
Lucy Goodhart
Giles Goodland
Marc Goodman
Chris Gostick
Bella Grace
Christin Green
Devon Greene
Christoph Greger
Amanda Griffiths
Jay Griffiths
Jennifer Gruenhagen
Andrew Grundon
Erica Guinn
Dorothy "Peaches" Gulino
Linda Haczyński
Kelly and Chris Haegglund
Julia Haltrecht
Allis Louise Hamilton
Rosie Hamilton
Stephen Hampshire
Cassie Hanback
Jo Hanlon-Moores
Zoe Hansen
Lynn Hardaker
Marisa Harder-Chapman
James Harleen
Faye Hartley
Finley S. Hauber II
Ruthie Hayes
Martin Hazell
Roger Heaton
David Hebblethwaite
Susan Hemann
D M Hemming
Jennie Heppenstall
Margaret Hess
Cecilia Hewett
Tamara A Hicks
Heath Hilary
Amber Hill
Yannick Hill
Charlotte Hills
Laurence Hills
Helen Hilton
Tom Hirons
Harrison Hobart
Jan Hobbins
Collin Hoctor
Louise Hoffman
Lydia Hoffman
Tania Hoffmann
Lisa Hofmann
Hilary Holden
Josephine Holt
Nick Hooper
Alexis Hopkins
Elizabeth Hopkinson
Stephen Hoppé
Julie Hornby
Philippa Howden
Adriana Hoyle
Simon Hughes
Nikki Humphreys
Kyle Hunter
Liz Hunter
Simon Hutchinson
Tim Hutton
Deb Ingebretsen
Johari Ismail
Rebecca Jackson
Indiana Jane
Toby Jeffries
Ellen Jenkins
Lisa Jenkins
David Jennings
JM
Jennifer Johnson
Amy Johnston
Mattie Joiner
Michael Jones
Siân Jones
Aerina Kamp
Kjartan Kári
Cynthia Keeely
Megan Keely
Hilary Kemp
Julia Davison Kemp
Aidan Kendrick
Lyn Kenny
Jan Kewley
George Khayat
Dan Kieran
Fuggo King
Steve King

SK Kirkham
Eilis Kitts
Catherine Klatt
Stephanie Knight
Carol Knorpp
Andreas Kornevall
Brian Koser
Moniczka Kowalczyk-Kroll
Carolyn Kristof
John Labovitz
Sara Lamb
Sarah Lambourne
Sienna Latham
Laura Lauff
Johanna Laun
Sarah Lawless
Alison Layland
Gregory Layshock
Molly Layshock
Annette LeClair
Kelsey Lee
Sophie Lee
Tammie Lee
Rebecca Lefebvre
Matt Leivers
Leslie Lekos
Kyle Lemle
Lynn Lemyre
Mona Lewis
Louise Lieb
Judith Lindquist
Tara Quinn Lindsey
Christine Linfield
Daniel G Linsteadt
George Linsteadt
Julia Linsteadt
Ken Linsteadt
Lyda Linsteadt
Simon Linsteadt
Stephen Linsteadt
Rodney W. Livingston
Kim Locke
Ann Loker
Annie-Rose London
Penelope M Long
Charlie Lord
Melody Lorraine
Mezzie Elen Lucerne-Lambourne
Brigitte Colleen Luckett
Jenn Lui
Julia Macintosh
Becky Mackeonis
Heidi and James Mackey
Demariea Mallon
Hilary Manning-Morton
Mike Marinos
Melanie Maroney
Clint Marsh
Craig Marshall
Fiona Marshall
Frances Marshall
Ben Martin
Susan Marynowski
Wade Mashburn
Lawrence Maskill
Christina Mathis
Bob Mayfield
Martina Mazzanti
Clare McAlpine
Molly McClure
Cheryl McCord
Addie McDermott
Betsy McDermott
Fiona McDiarmid
Molly McEnerney
Nion McEvoy Jr.
Kate McGillivray
Becky McGinnis
Gavin McGregor
Jenny McIntosh
Bridget McKenzie
Catherine McKinney
Cathleen McMahon
Andrew McMillan
Wendell McMurrain
Marie McNeil
Laurie McNeill
Niki na Meadhra
Claire Mehling
Lara Mehling
Wolf Mehling
Agnes Metzger
Jonathan Migliori
Jenny Miller
Sally Mineur

Hannah Mintz
Susan Minx
John Mitchell
John Mitchinson
Cynthia Mollenkopf
Matthew Mollenkopf
melita mollohan
Avonda Monotropa
Ivy Moon
Mab Moon
Serenity Moonflower
Andrea Moore
Claire Moore
Bethan Morgan
Paula Morgan
Dianna Morris
Jean Morris
Natalie Mulford
Stephanie Mulholland
Tom and Anne Mundahl
Rosie Murray
Matt Murrell
Wade Myslivy
Izzy Nance
Reni Narayen
Stu Nathan
Carlo Navato
Karen Nease
Lyndsey Neate
Diana Nelson & John Atwater
Elise Newbury
Elinor Newman
Julie Nicholson
Abi Nielsen
Jennette Nielsen
Abby Nolan
Emily Nolan
Jo Norcup
John Norton
Ashley Nunez
Havilland O'Briant
Rodney O'Connor
Penn O'Gara
Judith O'Grady
The Oppenheim Family
Eva Orbuch
Mat Osmond
Leora Pangburn
Tena Parkinson
Carla Parrott
Seema Patel
Diane Paterson
Valorie Paul
Emma Payne
Sylvie Pearson
Greetje Penning
Rob Percival
Lori Perlman
Abigail Perrow
Laura & Amanda Perry
Aileen Peterson
Erin Piorier
Jessica Pizzo
Harriet Platts
Susan Plott
Philip Podmore
Claire Podoll
Heather Podoll
Katherine Podoll
Samantha Podoll
Dave Pollard
Justin Pollard
Beth Pollins
Audrey Pondek
Joie Power
Milla Prince
Donald Proud
Georgina Pugh
Tam Purkess
Lisa Quigley
Jonny Randall
Morgen Raney
Sam Rawlings
Timo W. Bravo Rebolledo
Penny Reed
Penny Reilly
Mason J. Relyea
Noah S. Relyea
Fred Relyea III
Kay & Fred Relyea Jr.
Rebecca Rennie
Erin Reschke
Carolyn Reynolds
Kathleen Rice
Scott Richardson-Read

Liam Riley
Esme Roads
Adrienne and Bryan Roberts
Imogen Robertson
Ali and Dirk Robertson-Grundon
April Robinson
Hal Robinson
Lucinda Robinson
Claire Robson
Cinnamon Rose
Kiva Rose
Sophia Rose
Caroline Ross
Shelly Ross
Lucy Rossi
Harry Rotsch
Julie Ruskin
Lucy Ryder
Imogen Di Sapia
Yaga Sara
Andrew Sargent
Clare Sargent
Riccardo Sartori
Rachel Sater
Sunny Savage
Caroline Scanlan
Kat Scanlan
Monika Schmid
Cynthia Schmidt
Hannah Schmitt
Lisa Schmitz
Alexis Schroeder
Nell Scott
Jackie Sealey
Sealife of the Sea
Nikiah Seeds
Lindsey Segerberg
Bell Selkie
Katherine Setchell
Nikki Shabbo
arLene Shannon
Hank Shaw
Karen Shephard
Shorny
Kev Sibbald
Elizabeth Silvolli
Caitlin Simons
Nao and Mark Sims
Jane Singer
Sole Sisters
Linda Slack
Larkin F. Small
Helen Smee
Karen Smidth
Stephanie Byrd Smith
Teresa Squires
Maria Staines
Pamela Staines
Jeanine Starritt
Jenny Steer
Mark Stefanski
Patti Steinbruner
David Stevens
Lisa Stockley
Mags Phelan Stones
Pernille Strande
Dougie Strang
Leann Strobel
Asia Suler
Gail Sulikowski-Lopez
Jill Sullivan
Melissa Sylvan
Susan Tait
Sarah Tanburn
Alice Tarbuck
Asrik Tashlin
Shirley Taylor
Jillian Tees
Amanda Terry
Sarah Thomas
Amanda Thompson
Terry Thygesen
Paul Tompsett
Bernard Trainor
Judith Tripp
Aoife Troxel
Jane True
Joan Tucker
Simon Tume
Tracey Turner
Lucinda Tyler
Ruby Tuesday Udy
Charlie Umhau
Creel Forever Unbelove'd
Cara Usher

Kate Vagabond
Saskia van Herwaarden
Bethany van Rijswijk
Charles Vane
Alexis VanHorn
Sophie Vener
Mark Vent
Susan Ventura
Elis Vermeulen Vermeulen
Andrew & Dorothy Victor
Jean Victor
Joe Victor
Lisa Victor
Cherie Visconti
Annette & Wolfram von Specht
Phoebe Vreeland
Steve Wadsworth
Lisa Wagner
Della Walker
Mara Wallace
Nick Walpole
Meredith Walsh
Lawrence Wang
Mark Warder
Lucas Warford
Glory Warner
Constance Washburn
Olivia Watchman
Aly Waterfall
Louise Watson
Gayle Wattawa
Lucy Webb
Gregory Webster
Linden Weiss
Karen Wessel
Robin Borgers Whealdon
Herbert Wheeler
Kathleen White
Terry White
David Whiteside
Patricia Whitworth
Jessica Wick
Rush Wickramasinghe
Mary Widdison
Khristin Wierman
Angela Willard
Emma Williams
Liz Williams
Regina Williams
Sheila Williamson
Angie Willis
Lana Marie Willow
Derek Wilson
Miriam Wilson
Preston Wilson
Amy Winchester
Terri & Howard Windling-Gayton
Linda Winn
Cynthia Winton-Henry
Paul V. Wiseman
Chiquita Woodard
Simon Woodard
Spencer Woodard
Lulu in the Woods
Jane Wren
Jennifer Wright
Susan Wuorinen
Mark Yanover
Jackie York
James Young
Susan Zasikowski